"I've been waiting a week for this,"

Kurt said in a voice that was deep, husky and barely audible.

With his palm against her cheek, he turned her face up, then lowered his lips to hers. There was nothing tentative in the kiss, nothing questioning or hesitant.

When his arms closed around her, Gillie realized she, too, had been longing for this. Every nerve in her was awakening with feelings she had long ago forgotten.

Wonderful feelings.

All this time she had thought she didn't miss them.

She had thought she could live without them.

She had been wrong.

Dear Reader,

Welcome to the Silhouette **Special Edition** experience! With your search for consistently satisfying reading in mind, every month the authors and editors of Silhouette **Special Edition** aim to offer you a stimulating blend of deep emotions and high romance.

The name Silhouette **Special Edition** and the distinctive arch on the cover represent a commitment—a commitment to bring you six sensitive, substantial novels each month. In the pages of a Silhouette **Special Edition**, compelling true-to-life characters face riveting emotional issues—and come out winners. Both celebrated authors and newcomers to the series strive for depth and dimension, vividness and warmth, in writing these stories of living and loving in today's world.

The result, we hope, is romance you can believe in. Deeply emotional, richly romantic, infinitely rewarding—that's the Silhouette **Special Edition** experience. Come share it with us—six times a month!

From all the authors and editors of Silhouette **Special Edition**,

Best wishes,

Leslie Kazanjian,
Senior Editor

VICTORIA PADE
Twice Shy

Silhouette Special Edition

Published by Silhouette Books New York

America's Publisher of Contemporary Romance

SILHOUETTE BOOKS
300 East 42nd St., New York, N.Y. 10017

ISBN: 0-373-09558-9

First Silhouette Books printing October 1989

Printed in the U.S.A.

Books by Victoria Pade

Silhouette Special Edition

Breaking Every Rule #402
Divine Decadence #473
Shades and Shadows #502
Shelter from the Storm #527
Twice Shy #558

VICTORIA PADE,

author of both historical and contemporary romantic fiction, is the mother of two energetic daughters, Cori and Erin. Although she enjoys her chosen career as a novelist, she occasionally laments that she has never traveled beyond Disneyland, instead spending all her spare time plugging away at her computer. She takes breaks from writing by indulging in her favorite hobby—eating chocolate.

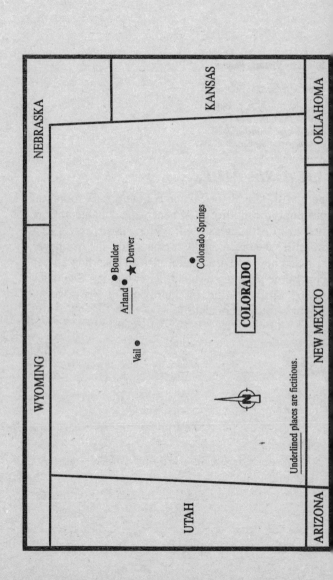

WYOMING

NEBRASKA

KANSAS

Vail •

Boulder •
Arland •★ Denver

COLORADO

Colorado Springs •

UTAH

Underlined places are fictitious.

ARIZONA

NEW MEXICO

OKLAHOMA

Chapter One

"Remember, no more pranks, kiddo," Gillian Hunter reminded her ten-year-old son as she pulled her station wagon into the parking lot at Conner Elementary School.

"Who me?" Elijah feigned innocence. He pulled his backpack up from between his feet, and the sound of jingling coins condemned him.

"Yes, you. And make sure you return every penny of that money."

"It's not fair," Elijah grumbled. "They got what they paid for."

"No more arguments," Gillie said firmly, narrowing her eyes at her towheaded son. "I've already heard about the fourth-grade girls willingly signing up for kissing lessons and how you were just offering them a service and what a great businessman you are because you kept books and gave credit. Just check those books, give the money back and keep your lips under wraps until you're eighteen. Got it?''

"Guess that means I don't have to give you a good-bye kiss then, huh?" He smiled impishly.

Gillie leaned over the gear shift and cupped her son's thin face in her hand. "Wrong." She kissed the tip of his nose, ignoring the grimace it inspired.

Elijah swiped the kiss away with the back of his wrist the minute Gillie let him go. "Oh, geez, there's Germy Best. He probably saw."

"His name is pronounced Jeremy," Gillie corrected. "And he kisses *his* mother goodbye."

"That's because he's a dweeb."

"You're just mad because it was Jeremy who informed on you."

"Wouldn't you be, if you were me?"

Since Gillie always tried to be honest with him she didn't answer, knowing her reply would be yes. Instead she said, "Make it a good day, Lijah. I'll see you this afternoon."

Elijah got out, but before closing the door he poked his head back in. "Make me peanut butter cookies?"

"Stay out of trouble and I'll think about it."

Gillie shook her head and smiled to herself as she watched her son cross to the sidewalk and join his friend Matt. Elijah's mischief was plentiful but never malicious. This year's shenanigans had involved rearranging the food in the cold lunch sacks, going to music class wearing a banana peel on his head, accepting a dare to check out the mysteries of the girl's bathroom, reading aloud in pig latin—and now this: kissing lessons.

"And it's only November," Gillie said aloud as she waited for her wiry, long-limbed son to enter the school.

However harmless, his pranks were still disruptive and it was the rare teacher who saw humor in the chaos of finding Elijah Hunter in her class. But so far Gillie's every attempt to channel his energies elsewhere had only left her frustrated.

"Look on the bright side," she told herself as she watched Elijah snatch a girl's earmuffs. "Maybe this is how Laurence Olivier or Albert Einstein were as a kids."

One of the other mothers got out of the car beside Gillie's and waved to her as she passed. Gillie waved back and then self-consciously smoothed her hair behind her ear. Ordinarily by the time she brought Elijah to school she had already had her bath, washed and combed her hair, and put on the light makeup that lasted her through the rest of the day. But on this crisp November morning Gillie had gotten out of bed at five to put the finishing touches on the artwork for an advertisement for tennis shoes. She had worked right up until it was time to leave. As a result she had barely combed her long sable-brown hair, she had hidden her unmascaraed topaz-colored eyes behind sunglasses and she was dressed in a sweatsuit that had been demoted to window-washing attire. She had been hoping no one would see her today.

Elijah disappeared into the school, and Gillie eased out of her parking place. She came to a stop behind a silver Corvette unloading two little boys. She noticed the vanity license plate: MYSTIC. Was the driver being clever or was it an announcement that he really did have a sixth sense?

"I could have used a mystic in my life a couple of times," she mused wryly to herself. "Boy, but what I would have been spared if I could have seen past the surface of some things. And some people."

The two boys closed the door on the Corvette and headed for the sidewalk. Gillie eased up on the brake and let her small station wagon inch forward. It took her a moment to realize that rather than also moving ahead, the Corvette was rolling backward. Instantly she pushed on the brake and came to a stop, but still the sports car rolled toward her.

"Stop, stop, don't hit me," she said as if it would make a difference.

But the distance between them kept closing.

In panic Gillie tried to hit the horn, missed and fumbled until she found it, finally ripping the peaceful morning apart with a loud blare.

The brake lights on the Corvette flared red; it stopped rolling and died.

Then out came Mystic's hand in an obscene gesture, followed by Mystic himself—a big, burly gorilla of a man who looked so mad Gillie thought smoke would have looked appropriate coming out of his ears.

A headline flashed through her mind: Divorced Ad Artist Killed In Grade School Parking Lot.

She tried smiling conciliatingly as she rolled her window down. A cold gust of late autumn air chilled her. "Sorry, but—"

That was as far as she got before Mystic shouted, "The damn starter's going out and it took two mechanics from my auto club to get that car going this morning. I'm already late for an important appointment and just because you're horn-happy—"

"You were rolling backward and were about to hit me," Gillie put in as he placed a fist on her windshield and bent his snarling face to her open window.

"You're full of it, lady. I know what I'm doing behind the wheel of a car, which is more than I'd bet on about any damn woman. It was probably you that was rolling into the back of me. For two cents—"

"Hey now, hold on," said a very deep voice from behind Mystic. "That's a lady you're talking to and there're impressionable kids all around here. A school parking lot is no place for this. And she's right, you were rolling backward."

Gillie watched Mystic straighten to his full height and still have to look up to meet the eyes of a man whose shoulders were about four inches broader to boot.

Mystic bellowed, "This isn't any of your business."

The other man's sharply angular jawline was set sternly above the starched white collar of the shirt he wore under a gray flannel suit. There was something about his attitude that reduced Mystic to a misbehaving child. "And this isn't getting your car started or you to that important appointment you said you were already late for. Why don't you see what you can do about that?"

Mystic sneered, looked the other man up and down, then went back to his car, but not without venting his anger with a hard punch to Gillie's fender.

Gillie hadn't realized how tense she'd been until Mystic was gone and she sat back against her seat. "Thank you," she said to the man in the gray flannel suit. He was watching Mystic, and Gillie couldn't help noticing how attractive his profile was. His hair was a dark, walnut-brown color, cut short at the sides and combed back neatly on top. His brow was strong, his nose narrow and straight. His lips were not too full and not too thin, and his cheekbones were prominent in a way that put him somewhere between rugged-looking and male-model perfect.

Somebody's father and more than likely somebody's husband, Gillie thought. But she noted the lines of his extraordinary face for the menswear ad she'd be drawing next month. In fact, she could use his whole body...for work. He was extremely tall, his broad shoulders in perfect proportion to his narrow waist and hips. His legs were long, and if the stretch of gray flannel over his thighs was any indication, they were muscular, too.

"You're welcome," the deep voice answered, and in a flash Gillie raised her eyes to the face that now stared at her. He was smiling and looked so disarmingly handsome that she felt heat rise all the way to her face. Or maybe the heat came from the sudden realization of how she herself looked. As if she could hide behind them, she pressed the sunglasses more firmly against her face.

"Everybody gets off to a bad start some mornings," the Parking-lot Hero went on in a tone that was at once kind, reassuring and somehow sexy. "Don't let his ruin the rest of your day."

Gillie reminded herself that the man was more than likely married. And that she was not interested regardless. "I'm just glad you stepped in before things got worse," she managed to say, glancing toward the Corvette that had started on the fourth try. It left tire rubber behind as it sped to the stop sign. "I guess it doesn't necessarily follow that being a mystic also makes him a nice guy." At the man's confused expression she nodded in the direction of the sports car. "The license plate."

The Parking-lot Hero followed her glance and laughed, a deep, rich sound. "I saw a vanity plate yesterday that said 'I Party.' It was on an old sedan driven by a tiny, sweet-looking white-haired lady going ten miles under the speed limit. She pulled into the turn lane and we came to the stop light next to each other. I glanced over and she gave me the most wicked, outrageous wink I've ever seen in my life."

Gillie laughed. "My favorite just said 'Oh Well.' I kind of like the idea of a license-plate shrug."

This time he just chuckled, but it was every bit as rich as his full laugh. "Yeah, I kind of like that, too."

His eyes were green, she noticed, a striking sea green shaded by lashes that were long and thick. For a *man* to have them proved there was no justice.

A car pulled up behind hers, and Gillie was grateful for the excuse to break off the conversation. "I better get going before somebody honks at me. Thanks again."

"No problem. I was on my way into the school anyway." He drew back from her car but stared at her as if he was about to say more.

Gillie waited expectantly. When he raised a hand and waved, she realized he was just waiting for her to leave before he crossed to the sidewalk. "Oh," she said to herself. Then she let out the clutch too fast and her car jerked to a stop. Feeling like an idiot and silently begging the engine to start, she cast a wan smile at the very attractive man watching her ineptitude. Somehow it seemed as if the situation would have been better had her hair been combed and her makeup on.

She turned the key. The engine purred back to life and Gillie knew a higher force had taken pity. Still feeling foolish, she stepped on the gas and pulled away, rolling her window up and wondering why she couldn't ever be smooth.

As she waited at the stop sign she glanced in her rearview mirror. The Parking-lot Hero had finally made it to the main entrance of the school. But before going in he stopped and turned to look in her direction.

Warmth flushed through her again. She reached to turn the heater off only to find it hadn't been on at all.

I must be coming down with something, she thought, then tore her eyes away from her rearview mirror and turned out of the parking lot.

Gillie lived on Muncie Avenue, a quiet street in the middle of the main housing development in Arland, a small suburban community half an hour's drive from Denver. Behind two giant oak trees her ranch-style house was part red brick, part gleaming white siding. The black shutters she had put on all the windows added a Colonial touch.

She pulled up her driveway and as she waited for the automatic shiny black garage door to open, Gillie caught sight of her next-door neighbor—who also happened to be her cousin and best friend—heading in her direction. It was no surprise. Robin Baumgardner's job as an insurance agent had flexible hours, and Gillie had figured this would be one morning her tall, stocky, blond cousin would want to catch her.

Robin waved as she waded through the ankle-deep autumn leaves in Gillie's yard. She followed the car into the garage. "I've been waiting for you," she said as Gillie got out.

"I figured you would be," Gillie teased her cousin. "I'm surprised you didn't call when you got home last night."

"I would have if your lights had been on. But they weren't and Danny said you had come home around nine. You didn't stay to mingle," the taller woman chastised as Gillie unlocked the door that led into the house.

Gillie chose not to answer. She merely placed her purse and keys on a small antique ice chest just inside the door, careful not to hit the basket of dried baby's breath that shared the oak top.

The door from the garage opened into a U-shaped space with the living room on one side and the dining room and kitchen on the other. Gillie rounded the drawing table in the dining room and went to the kitchen to make herself tea. Robin, as usual, had brought a cup of coffee with her.

"You couldn't have stayed for the socializing afterward if you were home by nine," her cousin reiterated, obviously expecting an explanation.

"Have a brownie," Gillie offered. She sat across from Robin and set down a half-empty plate of the sweets.

"Oh no," Robin groaned.

"Oh no?" Gillie repeated, confused.

"Look at those things." She pointed to the brownies. "*Triple* chocolate. Was the seminar that bad?"

"I didn't say that."

"You didn't have to. The color of what you're baking reflects your mood. When you're happy you bake with peanut butter, oatmeal, cinnamon or *milk* chocolate. But when you're unhappy or upset or nervous or depressed, everything that comes out of this kitchen is chocolate. And the darker the chocolate, the darker the mood. So let's have it. What happened last night?"

Gillie took a bite of a brownie, glad that Robin had no way of knowing she had eaten these smothered in hot fudge last night. "Next year for my birthday could you buy me a pair of flannel pajamas?"

Robin rolled her eyes. "I'd rather buy you transparent lingerie and know someone besides you will be seeing through it. You just turned thirty-three and you want me to buy you granny gowns. That's not healthy, Gil. Now, let's have it—every last detail of the How Singles Connect seminar."

Gillie took a sip of tea. "There were quite a few people."

"Strike one. Gillie the introvert immediately took a seat in the back and tried to hide."

If only that had been possible. "All the chairs were in a circle at first. Then we had to break up into groups of people with the same color clothes on, or with birthdays in the same season, or with the same size thumbs." She couldn't help the grimace at that last one. It had been intended as fun, but she felt like a jerk going around measuring thumbs with strangers. "Actually, thumbs were a theme for the evening. We had to touch thumbs with each person we talked to and give a one-finger wave before moving on."

Even Robin groaned at that. "So how did you do?"

"Well, let's see. One of the first things we were supposed to tell our groups was what our biggest accomplishment was. Just before it was my turn I choked on a swallow of tea and after coughing for what seemed like twenty minutes I said, 'Breathing.' No one laughed. Later on some guy who walked with a Popeye swagger and looked like he was carrying tennis balls in his armpits complained about summer being over and having to go to the tanning salon to get some color. I said I never went out in the sun so I didn't have to worry about my fan tading. He looked at me like I was nuts and it wasn't until I was in the next group that I realized I had said fan tading instead of tan fading. After that I just kept my mouth shut." Actually not long after that she had snuck out to the grocery store to do the week's shopping and save herself the chore today. But Robin didn't need to know that.

"Fan tading?" Robin repeated amid her laughter.

Gillie laughed, too, and then said, "If I cry uncle will you stop trying to matchmake me?"

"No." Robin didn't even bother to lie. "This stuff is all good for you. It hones your social skills."

"That's the point—I don't have any. You know I just clam up and sweat. I'm no good with new people." Oddly it occurred to her that she hadn't done that this morning with the Parking-lot Hero. She had talked to him as easily as if she had known him a long time. Without choking, stammering, stuttering, or even transposing letters.

"Besides," she went on when Robin finally stopped laughing, "you keep setting me up in these singles' situations and I'm hopeless at it. I just don't know the scripture of savvy. I still eat spaghetti instead of pasta. I watch movies instead of films. I can't be fluent in tennis shoe—is it Nike or Nietzsche? I never know whether the conversation is about sports of philosophy. I spell phonetically. How can I survive BMWs, CEOs, ASAPs, MBAs, TGIFs, FYIs, and MSGs, let along Früzen Gladje and Häagen Daz? Give me a break, Robin," she finished with a near shriek.

"I just don't want to see you alone," her cousin said more seriously.

"I'm not alone. I have Elijah and Rik."

"Rik is an obnoxious dog and Elijah will grow up and have a life of his own. Where will you be then?"

"How do I know?" Gillie said in frustration. "I don't even know where I'm going to find the time to rake leaves, let alone have a relationship, even if you *did* connect me to a man who knocks me off my feet."

What on earth caused the image of the Parking-lot Hero to come to mind at exactly that moment?

Gillie ate another brownie.

"If you had a husband you'd have someone to rake the leaves for you," Robin informed her smugly.

Gillie narrowed her eyes and said, "Maybe a big wind will come up and blow them all into your yard."

"I'm only interested in fixing you up," Robin defended herself, standing up to leave.

"I'm not broken down."

"And I'm not giving up. My goal is to see you happily married."

"Whether I like it or not." Gillie sighed and forced a less frantic, frustrated tone to her voice. "I really don't want any of that in my life again, Robin. I know your being happily married to Bob leaves you thinking that's the only way to live, but it just isn't. And I have absolutely, positively, gone to my last seminar and blind date and anything else you make me feel guilty enough to do. I mean it."

Just then the phone rang, which gave Robin the perfect excuse to ignore everything Gillie had said.

"Better answer that. I'll let myself out."

With her frustration renewed, Gillie picked up the phone. She instantly recognized the voice of Bob Baumgardner, Robin's husband and Elijah's school principal, on the other end. Wishful thinking made her say, "If you're looking for Robin she just left."

"I'm not. I'm calling about Elijah."

So much for wishful thinking. Gillie closed her eyes and held her breath for a moment. "Let me guess. He's holding the school nurse hostage until the cook promises to serve milk shakes with lunch every day."

"As a matter of fact I'm calling about a preventive measure before that one occurs to him."

"I'm against lobotomies, Bob," she deadpanned.

"I was thinking more of a big brother."

"You mean as in Big Brothers of America?"

"Not quite that structured. This would be a private agreement. After the kissing incident, I had a long talk with the school psychologist about Lijah. She seems to think his behavior might improve with some one-on-one attention from a man who's all his, so to speak. It isn't that I don't love having him with me and the twins. But the arrangement I'm thinking about would give him concentrated attention and maybe curb some of his need for the mischief that's garnering it for him now. Besides, after this kissing thing I'm a little worried that the company of my two seventeen-year-olds is too advanced for Elijah's own good."

"You have a point."

"I also have a volunteer. His name is Kurt Reynolds."

"Where have I heard that name?"

"He's the new principal at Arland High."

"Ah, now I remember. And since budget cuts and low enrollment threatened to cut the high school football program he took over coaching and you're assisting."

"He's the one."

"And he's willing to play big brother to Lijah?"

"He has some things going on in his own life that are frustrating his paternal instincts. And now that football season is about over he'll have time on his hands. I thought this might kill two birds with one stone."

"At this point I'm willing to try about anything to curb Elijah's mischief."

"Short of lobotomy," he reminded with a laugh.

"Just barely."

"Can you come to the school today about four? I'd like you to meet him before we set anything up formally."

"Sure. I'll be there."

Gillie hung up. The moment the phone was out of her hand her usual overprotective thoughts struck.

What if hidden behind the high-school principal's sterling reputation was really a child molester? What if he drove off with Elijah and her son's picture would have to appear beside the words Have You Seen Me? and Date Missing? What if Kurt Reynolds belonged to some religious cult and he brainwashed Lijah into worshiping white raisins?

These days a mother couldn't be too careful.

Maybe she should call Bob and tell him she didn't think this was such a good idea.

Gillie thought about what she would say. When she couldn't come up with a way not to sound like a lunatic she decided her imagination was running away from her. It was a malady she had contracted on the delivery table, something she made a conscious effort to control. This time control came with the reminder that Kurt Reynolds was a man Bob knew and trusted, a man she herself would interview this afternoon.

She headed for the bathroom, vowing to be optimistic. Maybe it would work, and the elementary school would still be standing by the time Elijah went on to junior high.

A cold November wind blew straight through Gillie's tweed coat as she locked her car door and headed to the elementary school that afternoon. With her collar turned up, her mouth and nose hidden behind a red muffler and her hands in her pockets, she hurried to Bob's office.

"Gillie, we were just wondering where you were," Bob called to her from behind his desk. He was a big, barrel-chested man with a round face. What was left of his hair formed a wreath around the shiny scalp of his head, making him look much older than he was.

"I'm sorry if I'm late," she said as she went in. "I had to take Elijah to a friend's house on the way and he was so busy telling me about meeting Mr. Reynolds this morning before school that I couldn't get him out of the car." She glanced at the other man in the room, her hands stopping midway in unwrapping her muffler.

There towering beside her was the Parking-lot Hero.

"Oh," she said inanely, suddenly feeling as foolish as she had that morning when she had blundered her getaway. Then she made it worse by adding, "It's you."

He smiled, and those green eyes of his took her in from head to toe. Gillie took a quick inventory of herself. This time her hair was French-braided and though she hadn't done anything special with her makeup and wished she had put on fresh blush, she knew her face had some color at least.

The deep voice she had remembered too many times that day sounded then. "It could be worse. It could have been Mystic."

That made her laugh.

Bob cleared his throat. "I take it that's a private joke. Do you know each other?"

The Parking-lot Hero answered, his gaze still on Gillie. "Not exactly. I had to rescue some poor guy on my way in here this morning before she flattened him."

He winked at her and Gillie's stomach jumped.

"I don't think I understand, but as long as you two do, I guess it doesn't matter. Why don't you take your coat off and sit down, Gillie?"

Odd how hard it was to extract herself from the penetrating gaze of the Parking-lot Hero. For crying out loud, pull yourself together, Hunter, she admonished herself.

She finished unwrapping her muffler and unbuttoned her coat, wondering why her fingers hadn't been this unco-operative out in the cold. Not until she sat in one of the chairs facing Bob's desk did both men reclaim their seats.

"Apparently you didn't know it before, but this is Kurt Reynolds. Kurt, this is Elijah's mother, Gillian Hunter."

"I should have guessed that the school mischief-maker had a mother mischief-maker."

"That's me all right." It seemed as if Kurt Reynolds was flirting with her and it made her very uncomfortable. She consciously guided the conversation back on track. "Elijah was excited about the prospect of having a big brother."

Bob jumped in. "I thought you'd go for the idea and since I'd asked Kurt to stop by on his way to school this morning to talk this over, it seemed practical to introduce them while I had them both here—even though I hadn't gotten the okay from you yet."

"Well, the idea and Mr. Reynolds both made a big hit." She didn't want to chance falling into Kurt's gaze again, but just to be polite, she shot him a very brief look. "Have you ever done this sort of thing before?" she asked as she picked nonexistent lint from her black stirrup pants.

"No, not really. I've worked with kids since before I graduated from college, coached little league baseball and football in the schools, but this is the first time I've done something like this."

"Do you have kids of your own?" Gillie was sliding the sleeves of her turtleneck sweater up to her elbows when she realized there was a beat of silence before he answered.

"I have a daughter but since her mother and I divorced she's lived with my ex-wife in Connecticut."

Frustrated paternal instincts, she remembered Bob saying on the phone that morning.

"Do you have ideas for the sort of things you'd be doing with Elijah?" It was getting awkward talking to him without looking at him so she stared at his tie.

"Since Bob just presented this arrangement to me this morning I can't say I've given it a lot of thought. But basically I see it as doing whatever any father would do—taking him to ball games, helping him with his homework if he needs it, going to a movie now and then, listening to him when he wants to talk. I thought we could just wing it. I imagine Elijah probably has an idea or two about what he'd do if he had a dad of his— Sorry, that didn't come out right. It's just that Bob told me Elijah hasn't seen his father in five years and that he's been tagging along with Bob and his sons rather than choosing what he might like to do."

Gillie wondered what else Bob had told him, then said, "Elijah's always full of ideas, all right."

"And of course you would have approval," Kurt assured her.

"So what do you think, Gillie?" Bob put in.

What *did* she think? Gillie wondered. She thought that Kurt made her feel odd.

Was it a warning to protect her son? Or some hormonal thing that didn't involve being Elijah's mother? Hard to tell since she hadn't felt like anything but a mother in so long.

But being around this man was the weirdest thing. She didn't have her usual tongue-tied, forget-her-own-name discomfort. And yet what she did feel was a new strangeness.

There was no understanding it.

But it wouldn't be fair to deny Elijah a friend who could very well be good for him just because Kurt Reynolds made her feel weird.

She finally answered Bob's question. "I think that if Elijah likes Mr. Reynolds and Mr. Reynolds liked Elijah and wants to take him on, it's fine with me."

"Then let's be on more familiar terms. Most real big brothers aren't called 'mister,'" Kurt said.

"That makes sense." Gillie smiled his way, hoping it camouflaged the fact that she still wasn't looking in his eyes. "Well, when would you like to start?"

"How about tomorrow evening? I have two tickets to a Nuggets basketball game. The only problem is that it might be a little late for him. I doubt if the game will end before ten."

Looking at Bob, she asked, "There isn't any school the next day, is there?"

"That's right, Thursday we're having a city-wide teachers' conference."

"As long as he can sleep late the next morning I don't think there's a problem."

"Great. Then I'll give Elijah a call tonight and invite him myself."

"He'd like that," Gillie said, knowing it was true. Sad to say, Kurt had been right about Elijah's being a tagalong to Bob's outings with his sons. Elijah was always a welcome tagalong, but a tagalong just the same. A special invitation all his own would thrill him. "I'll give you the phone number."

"Bob already has." Kurt stood up. "I'm afraid I have to run. I have an appointment with a parent in a few minutes. It was good to meet you—both times today." He extended his hand.

She didn't have a choice but to take it, and it was as unnerving as she had been afraid it might be. The contact sent little charges up her arm. Too quickly she pulled her hand away and tried to camouflage her uneasiness with gratitude. "I really do appreciate this," she said more effusively than she had intended to.

"I'm sure I'll enjoy it as much as Elijah will." He paused for just a beat before adding, "And I hope you and I can keep in close contact . . . to be sure I'm covering the bases with him and helping out wherever I can."

Was she just imagining it or had his voice become more intimate? It must be her imagination. Still, the effect left Gillie needing to clear her throat before she could answer him. "I'll certainly want to know how he's behaving." Then, all on their own, her eyes raised to his handsome face and once more got lost in those perfect lines.

"I'll see you tomorrow night, then. When I pick up Elijah."

"Sure." Gillie went back to studying his tie, wishing he would let go of her hand.

He finally did and turned to say goodbye to Bob.

After he had left, Bob repeated, "Well, what do you think?"

"He seems like a nice enough man," Gillie hedged.

"And he's single and unattached. I've kept him under wraps since I met him. I wanted to make this match myself and beat Robin to the punch just once. Even the boys were in on this one. We pointed out to her the other father that's helping coach the football team and said he was Kurt—a pudgy guy about an inch shorter than you are. Wait until Robin finds out who Kurt Reynolds really is and that I'm the one who introduced you."

Now this was familiar territory. Gillie gave a small, frustrated groan. "You're as bad as Robin."

Bob just smiled.

"Why can't I convince you Baumgardners that I'm just not interested? What's the saying? Once burned twice shy? Well, I'm twice burned, four times shy. Or maybe six or eight times shy since both burnings were hardly run of the mill stuff."

"Who are you kidding? You're just plain shy. Besides, you have it all wrong. The adage that applies here is third time is a charm."

"Bob, is this guy going to be good for Elijah or are you sacrificing my son on the altar of a matchmaking competition?"

"Want his vital stats? The man has a Ph.D., that makes him *Doctor* Reynolds. He was a star quarterback in college, could have made millions playing pro ball. He turned it down in favor of more education and working directly with the kids he could have just signed autographs for. Arland High got him because he wanted a grassroots type school where he could roll his sleeves up and dig in rather than just be a removed authority figure whose job is ninety-nine percent administrative. And on top of all that he's the most down-to-earth, unaffected, plain old good guy that I've ever met."

"In other words, he will be good for Elijah."

"He wouldn't be bad for you, either, Gil."

"I'm only interested in what he can do for my son." She already knew what he did to her and it was definitely not good. Gillie stood and put her coat on. "You wouldn't have embarrassed me by letting him in on your matchmaking intentions, would you?"

"Of course not. We've only talked about Lijah. I didn't go into anything that had to do with you so you don't have to look at me like that. And as for the matchmaking, he seemed pretty interested all on his own."

Gillie chose not to comment on that. "Don't say one more word to me or to Kurt Reynolds about any kind of romantic connection between him and me."

Bob held his hands up, palms out. "Hey, I've done my part. I'm just going to sit back and let nature take its course."

"Nature has already taken its course, in my experience an erratic, bumpy, painful one. Lucky for me I have my life on track now in spite of it. I absolutely do not want any surprises messing things up again."

"It is possible to have *good* surprises, you know."

"But highly unlikely and I'm not interested in taking the risk ever again." Gillie plunged her hands into her pockets. "Now if only I can get some goods on Robin and blackmail her into backing off, I can be a happy woman for the rest of my life."

"Okay, okay, I get the picture. But I still think Kurt will be good for Elijah."

"And for that I appreciate your efforts. Now I'd better pick my little devil up before he uses Matt's new doctor kit to operate on their cat."

Outside, Gillie poked her nose above her muffler. It seemed as if the temperature had dropped ten degrees, but now the cold air felt good. It made her realize that the heat Kurt Reynolds had inspired had lingered even after the man had gone. A bad sign.

Nature taking its course?

"Just leave your mitts off me, Nature, do you hear?" she said as she unlocked the car door and got in. "I don't want any more to do with you."

Chapter Two

It was after eight that night when Kurt finally got home. Juggling his keys, his dry-cleaned clothes, a fast-food bag that held dinner, three library books on child psychology and early childhood development, and the day's mail, he unlocked the security door to his apartment building. Then he climbed three flights of stairs, smiling as he passed the elderly man who lived next door coming out with his trash.

"Hello, walls," he said facetiously as he went into his own small two-bedroom apartment. It was almost as frigid as the air outside so he turned the thermostat up. Immediately the heat came on, not only adding warmth, but sound, a welcome interruption to the silence of an empty place.

He crossed to the television and turned it on. It wasn't that he wanted to watch anything, but like the sound of the heat, he welcomed the noise.

When the apartment was warm enough, he took off his coat, jacket and shoes, and sank down on the sofa. He laid out two cheeseburgers, fries and a vanilla milk shake on the coffee table, using their wrappers as plates.

He'd have rather had a thick slice of roast beef, mashed potatoes and gravy, salad, rolls and pie with coffee for dessert. But it had been a choice between staying dressed up and sitting in a restaurant alone or eating in his stocking feet. Comfort had won out.

As he ate, Kurt thumbed through his mail. When he came to a thick, satiny envelope, he set his cheeseburger down and opened the envelope, finding an invitation to the December wedding of an old friend.

"I can't believe you're doing it again," he said with a shake of his head. "This is the fourth time, Tom. Are you just going to keep trying until you get it right? Well, thanks but no thanks. I'll stick with eating fast food by myself until I find the right woman. No trial and error for this guy."

He slid the invitation to the corner of the table and picked up the last piece of mail, at the same time lifting three French fries to his mouth. His hand stopped when he realized who this letter was from.

"Ah, speaking of error."

The letter was addressed in a large and ornate handwriting that overwhelmed the business-size envelope.

"Hello, Carol," he said with as much enthusiasm as he had greeted his walls. Then he dropped it, unopened, on top of the bills, flyers and coupons.

Suddenly he realized he wasn't hungry anymore. He leaned back and glared at that Connecticut-postmarked envelope.

He didn't have to open it to know what was in it. His ex-wife had called last week and there was no doubt in his mind that this was just the follow-up.

"Nothing is ever enough for you, is it, Carol?" he asked the envelope. "Too bad I didn't see that fourteen years ago. But then I was twenty-one, idealistic and naive enough to believe you were, too." He paused. "Or maybe I was just too stupid to realize the difference between idealism and living in a dreamworld with every intention of making those fantasies become realities at any expense."

Kurt's glance caught the snow-white teddy bear sitting on a bookshelf of the oak unit that lined his wall. Sadness stabbed him.

Carol's desire for prestige and a storybook life that made the society pages hadn't come out until after they were married. When Kurt hadn't lived up to it she had gone in another direction to get it. And get it she had. But in her opinion, that image was marred by the existence of an ex-husband. In short, Kurt was the skeleton in her closet that she didn't want let out. And since there was nothing she could do legally to deny him his rights, she had mounted another campaign to get what she wanted.

He laughed mirthlessly. "It wasn't enough that two and a half years ago you took my six-month-old daughter clear the hell to Connecticut before she and I could even get to know each other. It wasn't enough for you to put every conceivable obstacle in the way of my visiting her. Now you want to use April's phobia to get me out of the picture completely."

April was a timid child, scared to death of strangers. And a stranger was just what her mother had made sure Kurt was to her. He visited every chance he had, but he never forced the issue by insisting she leave her mother and come to stay with him. Instead he just kept hoping this was a stage April would outgrow. But so far it had only gotten worse. Now Carol was pressing the point. And the guilt Kurt felt at being one of the causes of frightening his own child was giving weight to Carol's argument. He could only hope there was some kind of answer for him in the books he had just checked out.

The whole issue was on his mind so much lately that he had confided in Bob. That was what had inspired the idea of becoming Elijah's big brother. Bob had suggested that it might not only help Elijah, but be a tonic for Kurt, as well.

"God knows I'm a frustrated father," he said to himself.

He was really looking forward to spending some time with Elijah. The boy was ornery and full of the devil, and in all of Kurt's years of teaching he had always liked those kids the best. Bright and quick and imaginative, they were the most fun, the most interesting, the most challenging.

But it wasn't Elijah's face that popped into Kurt's mind. It was Elijah's mother's. And for some reason that made Kurt smile.

His ex-wife wouldn't have been caught dead looking the way Gillian Hunter had that morning. On her deathbed Carol would be calling for a pedicure. But rather than looking unkempt, Kurt had thought Gillie looked desirably mussed up and fresh-faced. He wouldn't have guessed her to be the mother of a ten-year-old. Then this afternoon, with that shiny hair of hers braided, her peaches and cream skin rosy from the cold, and those bright gold-flecked eyes of hers, she had looked as wholesome and down to earth as someone who belonged on a Connecticut farm.

Kurt had to laugh. Contrary to what Carol thought, by the time she was finished with hairdressers, manicurists, designers and makeup professionals she looked more as if she belonged in a New York penthouse. But rosy-cheeked Gillian Hunter looked the part of a country-estate owner.

Kurt wondered why one thought of Gillian Hunter wiped away his feeling frustrated, mad and just plain rotten, and raised his spirits.

She was attractive, naturally beautiful. And he had admired her equanimity in the face of that goon charging her like a bull this morning. To have come out of that with her sense of humor intact was like frosting on the cake. And there was definitely no affectation to her, in fact her lack of—of what? Aplomb? Sophistication?—was refreshing.

She was funny and fresh-faced.

"All right, so maybe I won't mind getting to know both mother *and* son," he said to the wedding invitation. "But that doesn't mean I'm like you, Tom. I'll be pretty damn cautious before I ever do marriage again."

Colorado's notoriously changeable weather brought sunshine the next day rather than the snow that had been predicted. Gillie viewed it as a reprieve. One snowfall on top of all those leaves in her front yard and she would have heavy wet mulch instead of nice dry leaves to rake up. But with her deadline finally met she could spare one day of yardwork before starting on her next assignment.

"Hurry up, Lijah, or you're going to be late," she called.

Gillie heard her son's muffled answer from the bathroom and braced herself. Elijah had spent most of last evening there, trying to get his hair to look like some rock star's.

"Get your tail out here now, Elijah Hunter," she said more firmly.

Elijah jogged down the hall, grumbling as he swept up his backpack. Obviously his hair experiment hadn't worked out too well—one side was slicked back but the other was sticking out over his ear. As he stomped past her into the garage she heard him mumble, "I can't wait till I'm old enough to shave my head."

"You'll never be that old," she told him as she slid behind the wheel of her car.

"Wow, did you come out and do that this morning already?" Elijah marveled as Gillie concentrated on backing up.

"Did I do what?" she asked.

"Rake the leaves," he explained, pointing.

Gillie glanced out her window, half expecting this to be one of her son's jokes. But sure enough the leaves that had fallen from both oak trees were in four neat piles near the massive trunks.

"Well, I'll be darned," she said to herself.

"It's like the shoemaker's elves," Elijah said to himself.

Gillie smiled. For all his attempts to seem older, Elijah was still just a little boy. "You think elves came and raked our leaves in the middle of the night?"

"Who else?"

"I don't know." She played along because there was so little magic he believed in anymore. "You must be right."

But Gillie decided it was Danny Baumgardner's handiwork. Last week the wilder of the Baumgardner twins had come to her for a loan to pay a parking ticket he didn't want his parents to know about. Teasing him, she had told him he could work it off by raking her leaves. Gillie hadn't really expected him to do it, both Danny and Brian were nice kids but they were in the throes of a whirlwind teenage social life. Robin was always complaining that they were worse about doing anything around the house now than they ever had been. It was a nice surprise to find that he had taken her seriously.

"Aw, come on," Elijah said dubiously. "You did it, didn't you?"

"Nope, I really didn't. I was going to do it when I got back from taking you to school this morning."

"Then who did it, do you think? It couldn't have been elves."

Gillie only faintly heard Elijah's question. Seeing those raked leaves made her recall an unpleasant memory. This was something her ex-husband had done in days gone by—surprise yardwork, leaf-raking in the night—as if it would make up for months of turmoil and worry and doubt and fear.

Old, ugly feelings flooded her as strongly as they had all those years ago. Her stomach turned inside-out, her throat constricted, and her chest became knotted with dread.

Silly, she chided herself. That was long past now.

"Come on, who did it, if you didn't, Mom?" Elijah demanded. "I know it wasn't elves."

The sound of her son's voice was a welcome call back to the present. Gillie shook off the flashback.

"I know you did it," Elijah persisted.

With some regret that his more worldly self had won out over his innocent side she answered him honestly. "I'm sure Danny did it before he went to school this morning. We made sort of a deal, I just didn't think he was going to come through." She cast another glance at those neat piles of leaves but refused to allow old, unwelcome thoughts to resurface. "And I'm really glad he did. It saves me a lot of work."

By ten that night the house was redolent with the cinnamon scent of fresh-baked apple pie. So that she wouldn't be spotted anxiously waiting, Gillie stood in the dark at Elijah's bedroom window, watching for Kurt's blue Volvo. A more in-depth interview was on her agenda for this evening and she didn't want to risk missing him in case he didn't walk Elijah to the door.

It wasn't that she didn't trust Bob's judgment. It was just that she would feel better about her son's relationship with Kurt Reynolds if she knew more about him herself. There hadn't been time before he and Elijah left for the game, but when they came home Gillie had the lure of pie waiting.

And a piece of it sent to bed with Elijah might forestall any embarrassing questions from her son about why she had changed into her new plaid blouse and washed and curled her hair.

At ten minutes after ten Kurt's car pulled into the drive. Gillie leaped over the train set in the middle of the floor and made a run for the living room.

By the time she got the front door open, Kurt and Elijah were on the porch. Her smile felt too big and Gillie tried to make it smaller as she held open the screen.

"You guys are just in time for a slice of hot apple pie," she said as if they were two boys coming in from play. She had rehearsed it in order to make it clear she saw Kurt only as Elijah's friend. And maybe if she was very convincing she could control her own unwanted thoughts about him as a man.

"Oh," Elijah moaned in ecstasy. "My mom makes the best apple pie. You have to have some," he said as he came into the house.

"You can have yours in your room while you get ready for bed." She looked at Kurt, trying not to notice how attractive he was in a turtleneck sweater, leather bomber jacket and tight, faded jeans. "Will you come in and have a slice?"

"Gee, Mom, are you sure it's okay?" he said with one eyebrow arched and the hint of facetiousness in his voice.

Gillie wasn't sure whether he was teasing her or letting her know he didn't appreciate her you-boys tone. She thought maybe both, and consciously upgraded the way she spoke to him. "I don't have any coffee but I could make you a cup of tea."

He gave her a lopsided smile, which seemed to signal his satisfaction over her getting the message that he was her peer and not Elijah's. "Just the pie would be good, thanks." He waited for her to step back into the living room, then followed. "It does smell good in here," he said, taking off his jacket and placing it over the arm of the blue sofa.

"How was the game?" she asked the room in general.

"Everybody good was on the injured list and we lost," Elijah said with so much enthusiasm he might have been announcing a wopping victory.

"I take it you had a good time anyway?" Gillie said, ruffling up his hair.

Elijah ducked out of her reach and let his own coat fall on the floor. "It was terrific."

"I'm glad. Say your thank-yous and head for bed. I'll bring your pie in in a few minutes. You can brush your teeth afterward."

It didn't take a second reminder for Elijah to thank Kurt. Gillie watched her son. He seemed completely at ease; camaraderie between him and Kurt was already blooming. She was glad to see that Bob had obviously been right about Elijah's need for a big brother type relationship. And she envied her son's relaxed attitude when she was feeling anything but.

"I want a big piece and a glass of milk," Elijah informed her.

"And all you have to do to get it is pick up your coat and take it with you."

When even that didn't raise a grumble Gillie knew the evening had been a success.

Then Elijah was gone and she was standing alone in her living room with Kurt Reynolds and sweaty palms.

"Sit down and I'll bring the pie," she suggested in a voice that didn't sound sure of itself.

"I'd rather help. I'm afraid I'm not used to sitting and being waited on. It makes me uncomfortable."

"There's nothing for you to help with, but if you want to come and watch you're welcome." The tension in her face must have shown that for the lie it was. The last thing she wanted was this man watching her do anything.

Begin the interview, she instructed herself on the way into the brightly lit kitchen.

"Do you come from a large family?" she blurted out too eagerly.

He didn't seem to notice as he crossed his arms over his chest and leaned his hips against the counter. "You're looking at the whole thing."

Was she ever. He was even more attractive dressed casually and with his hair less than perfect. Being a casual person herself, and always intimidated by suits, his appeal was only heightened. She concentrated on slicing the pie. "The whole thing?" she repeated a bit dimly.

"I was an only child and both of my parents are dead, my father when I was barely more than a baby and my mother a year ago."

"I'm sorry."

"So am I."

"It seems strange that you wouldn't have come from a big family," she observed as she took plates down from the cupboard.

"Why is that?" he sounded genuinely confused.

Gillie shrugged. "It's just that being an only child, Elijah is pretty adultlike. In a lot of ways he's more mature than the kids his age who have brothers or sisters, and he doesn't have a lot of patience with some of their childishness. I guess I picture people who really like kids, people who really relate to them the way you seem to, coming from big families."

"Well, I didn't. How about you?"

"Me?" She hadn't expected him to show any interest in her. It caught her off guard. "I have an older sister. She's married to a hog farmer in Kansas."

He was smiling when she glanced over at him and Gillie didn't know why. Was it because her sister was married to a Kansas hog farmer or because she was talking a mile a minute? She wiped her damp palms on her thighs before opening a drawer in search of the pie server. "Where did you work before coming to Arland?"

"I was headmaster at Lancaster Day School."

Gillie's eyebrows shot up in surprise. Lancaster Day School was the most expensive private school in Colorado. It didn't seem possible that anyone would leave a job like that voluntarily, and the way he'd said headmaster, as if it left a bad taste in his mouth, made Gillie wonder. Maybe his story about wanting a grassroots type of school had been a cover. She just had to ask. "Did you...uh...leave by choice?"

Kurt laughed. "I did. And you're not alone in thinking I must have been out of my mind to do it."

That wasn't what she was thinking but since it was so much nicer than what her paranoid mind was imagining she let him believe it. "Why did you? You must have taken an enormous pay cut."

"And I lost a guest membership at the Denver Country Club, too," he added with a laugh. "But those things were the least of my concerns. My father owned some real estate that was sold for a fair amount of money and my mother was a sharp investor who built what he left into enough to give me the freedom to do what I like regardless of the salary."

"What were the concerns that made you leave, then?" Gillie prompted.

"The kids. The headmaster of a private school has less to do with the students than the night janitor does. At least that was true of Lancaster. My job was to keep the parents who paid those outrageous tuitions happy, even if it was at the expense of what was best for their own kids. Unfortunately money can also create some pretty mixed-up values. I didn't get into education in order to be a yes-man to somebody who thinks a five figure balance in their checkbook should always get them their own way."

Okay, so the grassroots stuff might have validity. "Why did you get into education?"

"Because I believe in a pretty corny notion that kids are our future, that education—not money—is the most important asset any of us can have. And because I just plain like kids."

That reminded her of Bob's comment about Kurt's frustrated paternal instincts. "It must have been a terrible blow when your ex-wife moved your daughter out of state."

There was a split second before he answered. "To say that it was a terrible blow is an understatement. But she had her own agenda and I couldn't stop her."

Gillie felt tension in the air and she wondered why that happened with every mention of his daughter. But before she could question him further, he said, "So I went after the job at Arland High, where not only could I get involved with the kids again but even coach their football team. It seemed tailor-made for me."

"Arland is just this side of being a small town. It must be quite a change for you."

"You make it sound like five isolated farms and a combination gas station-grocery store-barber shop. It's not large, but it's still a suburban community, complete with all the amenities. We're only half an hour from Denver, and I haven't found any convenience I have to do without."

"Just wait until the first blizzard hits and it takes three days before our single snow plow clears your street and then does it by leaving a mountain of the stuff blocking the driveway you spent four hours digging out in the first place."

"Well, for the moment I'm renting one of the Oakwood apartments. Snow in the parking lot is their worry and since I'm only three blocks from my school I can walk to work. Another advantage of living in a small community."

Gillie turned to face him. "Excuse me, but I need a glass out of that cupboard behind your head."

He turned and opened the cupboard himself. "How big?" he asked, sounding as comfortable and relaxed with her as Elijah had seemed with him. Why was she the only one coming apart at the seams?

"Just a juice glass, thanks."

"One juice glass full of milk, coming up," he said, moving around her and opening the refrigerator door. Gillie's glance followed him. She was stunned by how at ease he was, yet at the same time she enjoyed the sight. Somehow his big masculine presence made her kitchen feel more homey.

Get back to the inquisition, Gillie, she ordered herself.

She picked up a plate with a slice of pie. "Speaking of where you live, while I take this into Elijah would you mind writing your phone number and address on the message board next to the phone? I realized after you had left tonight that if anything were to happen I wouldn't have that information to give to the police. I mean in case there was an accident and they needed to know—"

She'd blown it. She'd exposed her paranoia and she knew it. One glance at Kurt's face told her he knew it, too. He was grinning.

"Did you spend tonight thinking that I was going to abscond with your son and you wouldn't know where to even start looking?"

"No," she was too quick to deny it. "It's just—"

"Just in case I do," he finished for her, obviously amused.

"A person can't be too cautious," she said defensively after debating whether to deny her worries or tough it through honestly.

His eyes seemed to soften. "It's okay, no offense taken. You're right, a person can't be too cautious when it comes to their kids. I come up against too many parents who just don't care or won't take the time to know what's going on with them. I appreciate that you aren't one of those. In fact I find it admirable." He handed her Elijah's milk. "And I will write my address and phone number on your message board."

Gillie felt immensely better. Just the fact that he understood put her fears to rest. It proved he was very human behind that face and body that left her expecting him to be something more, something too elevated to relate to what a mother was thinking and feeling.

Now if only she could manage to feel like nothing more than a mother around him.

"When you're finished, why don't you take your pie out into the living room?" she said as she left with Elijah's share.

But five minutes later, after she had kissed her son goodnight, Gillie found Kurt sitting at the kitchen table, one piece of pie in front of him and the other waiting for her. He looked right at home and she had to admit that she preferred this to the more formal feeling of entertaining in the living room.

As she sat across from him, he lifted his chin in the direction of her next assignment posed beside her drawing table. "And what is it that you do that makes you put a shock absorber on a pedestal in what the architect who designed this house surely intended to be a dining room?"

"I'm an ad artist," she said after tasting her pie and discovering she couldn't enjoy it with so many things inside her on overdrive. "There's going to be a big promotion for that particular shock absorber, and I'm drawing it for the ads."

"Interesting," he said in a way that convinced her it was. "You're an artist."

Gillie shrugged. "There are those who don't consider it art. It's more aptly called illustration."

"And you do it free-lance?"

"Mmm."

"Is this something you always wanted to do or are you an aspiring Van Gogh just doing this to pay the bills?"

"Neither really. I actually didn't know anything about illustration when I started. I had a pretty useless degree in art and enough brains to know I was never going to be another Van Gogh. My ex-husband, before he was my husband at all, worked as a carpenter, specializing in remodeling. He had a job building a hot tub deck for the owner of the Neusman's department stores in Denver and he overheard Mr. Neusman talking about cutting costs by closing their in-house art department and hiring someone new to draw their ads, to give them a fresh look. Phil, my ex-husband, knew I could draw and since I was in need of a job at the time, he suggested me. I did some sketches, they went over big and I've been doing it ever since."

"Happily?" He was watching her intently and it made Gillie's mouth run away with her.

"Yes. Actually, I love it and I'm lucky to be able to work out of my home. It leaves my hours flexible so I can take Elijah to and from school and be here for him whenever he needs me. The only downside, at least according to Robin Baumgardner, is the isolation. I don't get out much and I almost never meet any new people." Gillie took another bite of pie even though she didn't want it. She didn't know any other way to stop this torrent of words.

"I already know you're divorced, but does part of this isolation mean you're not seeing anyone?"

His voice had suddenly dropped an octave and his tone was intimate. Gillie had a hard time swallowing. She said, "I see a lot of the Baumgardners and Elijah and everybody who frequents the grocery store."

"But you're not dating anyone?"

Little goosebumps were popping out on her arms. "No. Would you like another piece of pie?"

"No, thanks. But I would like it if you'd have dinner with me Saturday night."

"Did you want to talk about Elijah?" she asked, purposely being obtuse.

"I imagine he'll come up in the conversation. But what I really want is to get to know you. I haven't met a lot of women like you—"

"You just haven't been hanging out in the suburbs long enough." She cut him off because she didn't want to hear anymore. Her mind was working a mile a minute trying to figure out what to do.

"Give yourself some credit, Gillie."

Something about how he said her name in that deep baritone voice sounded like appreciation. None of Robin's candidates for a second husband had given her that impression. And no one had ever made her feel the way she did with Kurt Reynolds.

As she stalled by taking their plates to the sink, Gillie realized that there was a certain amount of safety in not having met a man who made her feel attractive or appreciated. It had saved her from feeling the way she did now, like some hormone-controlled teenager.

Stay safe, keep this guy at a distance, she advised herself.

"Listen." He came up beside her at the sink. "I think Elijah is a terrific boy. I enjoyed being with him tonight and I'm looking forward to spending a lot more time with him. But I also find you...interesting."

Interesting? It had been five years since she had felt like anything but Elijah Hunter's mom and that didn't seem too interesting. Still, it felt good to be considered that.

"How about it, Gillie?" His deep voice wrapped around her and drew her away from her thoughts. "Have dinner with me Saturday night. What better way to make sure that Elijah is in good hands than to get to know me?"

A good point. After all, that's why she had invited him in for pie. The more she knew about him, the better she could feel about Elijah spending time with him. And it would also probably take care of the bizarre reaction she had to the man. It wasn't that she wanted familiarity to breed contempt—this arrangement was too important to Elijah—but she would like it to breed imperviousness. Then Elijah could go off with his big brother, Gillie could rest easy while he did, and go back to her organized, uncomplicated, ordinary life.

"You're right," she conceded. "I do like to know all I can about anyone around Elijah. But it's only for this once and it isn't a date," she was quick to tell him.

His smile was slow and knowing. "So it has to be on those terms, does it? All right. I'll take your company any way I can get it. How about seven Saturday night?"

Gillie took a deep breath and wondered what on earth she was doing. "Seven would be fine."

His green eyes captured and held hers for a long moment. "I'll be looking forward to it," he told her softly.

"Nothing fancy, though. I don't like big deals."

"I didn't think you would. I'm glad I was right."

With his gaze still holding hers he smoothed a curl that had strayed to her temple. That scant contact sent an electric charge all through Gillie.

Then he pushed himself away from the counter and headed for the living room. She followed. "We can also set up a regular schedule for my seeing Elijah so he has that consistency to count on."

Elijah. Thinking about him was something concrete, something sane to hang on to. "From what I hear on the radio shrink show, that's important," she agreed.

She hadn't intended for that to be funny but he laughed anyway. Luckily it sounded kind and amused, not as if he was making fun of her.

"The radio shrink show?"

"A psychologist's radio program. I listen to her while I wait for Lijah to come out of school. She always says consistency and being able to count on people is the most important thing to a child, more important than a million dollars in toys."

"She's right," he said, watching her intently again, as if he was seeing something he didn't quite believe.

Gillie opened the front door because she needed a little cold November air to cool the warmth his eyes generated. "Thanks for taking him tonight. He seemed to have had a great time."

Kurt shook his head. "No thanks necessary. I had every bit as good a time. Saturday night at seven?" he repeated as he moved to the door.

He was standing very near to her, so near that she could smell the faintest hint of his after-shave. She tried not to like it so much. "At seven," she agreed, opening the screen door.

"See you then."

Gillie watched as he walked to his car. She kept on watching as he backed out of her driveway. She didn't close the door until he was halfway down the street.

And all the while she kept wondering how Elijah's mom had turned into this woman who didn't feel anything at all like a mother.

Chapter Three

"Knock, knock," Robin said, stepping into Gillie's bedroom on Saturday morning. "Good grief, did you get the name of the cyclone that came through here?"

"Vanity," Gillie answered. She stood in the center of the room amid clothes-strewn furniture.

"I get busy with appointments and don't see you for two days and look what happens." Robin surveyed the mess as she sipped the coffee she had brought with her.

"I need some help deciding what to wear tonight."

"So you said when you called a few minutes ago. I don't know that I want to contribute to this date."

"Now that's a switch. You're usually trying to contribute everything from the man on down. And it's not a date."

"But if you fall madly in love with this guy, marry him and live happily ever after, Bob will *never* let me hear the end of it. He says we're going for the world record in championship matchmaking."

Gillie picked up a pair of dark jeans and a chambray shirt and held them in front of her. "You can relax and give me your advice because there's no contest. I have not been match-made. Like I said, this isn't really a date."

Robin burst out laughing.

"I mean it." Gillie put down the chambray shirt and picked up a turtleneck sweater. But it had a snag across the front and she threw it on top of the pile on the arm chair. "This is not romance."

"Then celibacy has wreaked havoc with your brain cells. My dear old husband wanted to fully enjoy his joke so on Wednesday night he made me watch out the window for a glimpse of Arland High's newest head of staff. Kurt Reynolds is magnificent."

"As if anyone had to force you to look."

Robin leaned against the doorframe. "So, where are you going?"

"He said dinner, and I said as long as it was no big deal, so I'm expecting something simple."

Robin rolled her eyes. "I know, I know. Your philosophy that low expectations keep you from big disappointments. But if Kurt Reynolds is even half as good as Bob says he is you shouldn't be in for any disappointments at all. If I were you I would go for the Rattlesnake Club."

"*No one* is half as good as they seem. I should know."

"Lord knows you've seen the worst. But I still think you're a cynic."

"Uh-huh," she agreed.

"Okay, so you have good reason to be and I'm responsible for one of the two biggest causes in your life. But maybe this time..."

"Don't start with that guilt stuff or the maybe-this-time routine, Robin. Just tell me what to wear."

Her cousin shrugged and shook her head. "There's no choice, Gil. You own jeans and tops that you wear every day to work in and none of them are appropriate for this. Then you have your black wool pants and silk blouse which are too dressy for a low-expectations, no-big-deal dinner. That only leaves the gray slacks, white tuxedo blouse and black vest—the same thing you always wear."

Gillie looked at the outfit Robin had described where it hung from hangers on a doorknob. She grimaced at it. She had wanted to wear something different tonight, something more...striking. Then she realized that in itself was a bad sign. "Okay. The gray, white and black it is. Maybe I could wear a scarf or something."

"Oh great, another layer. Or maybe you could actually leave a few buttons undone instead of fastening the blouse up to your chin so you don't look like a librarian."

"That's how I achieve an air of mystery. I like to leave them wondering what's underneath that high-necked shirt."

"And that vest and those baggy pants and the blazer you usually wear over it all. What you really need is a guy with a great imagination.'' Robin paused a moment before asking with all teasing aside, ''What do you honestly think of this guy, Gil?''

Gillie shrugged as if it didn't matter. ''He seems nice. So far there's no sign of a big ego or the kind of arrogance that face could easily come with. It's kind of weird. I don't feel out of step or awkward or self-conscious with him,'' she finished almost more to herself than to Robin.

''Let me see if I have this right,'' her cousin said incredulously. ''You mean you actually remember his name when you're around him?''

Gillie nodded in disbelief herself.

''I'll never understand how someone so on top of things, so adept, so dependable, so in control, so . . . together in everyday life, turns into—''

''A mush brain,'' Gillie finished for her.

''The minute you get around a new man. But not with this guy, huh?''

''Not yet anyway. It'll probably set in.''

''Or it just isn't going to happen. Maybe all these years it's been some strange internal warning system you have. When you finally hit the right man it doesn't go off.''

''No, that can't be. It didn't go off with Phil or with Paul, and both times even low power instincts should have picked up some serious danger signals.''

''The hideousness of those two experiences are what started this happening, if you'll recall. Before them you were as adept a flirt as the rest of us. I think your unconscious instigated it to keep you out of harm's way until a really decent guy came into your life.''

Gillie opened her mouth to deny it yet again but her cousin cut her off before she'd made a sound. "I don't care what you say, this man has struck a chord. Bob gets points on this one even it isn't a match."

After her cousin had left, Gillie wondered about the chord Robin seemed to think Kurt had struck in her. She could deny it until the end of time but the truth was, she felt different with this man and it wasn't only those hot flashes he gave her. Reluctantly she acknowledged that she was attracted to him, that there was some chemical reaction between them. And it was all very unnerving.

But Gillie believed she knew the antidote to the attraction.

And she was putting it into effect by having dinner with him tonight.

When Kurt realized it was already six-thirty and he had nearly forgotten to make his Saturday evening phone call to his daughter, it occurred to him for the first time just how distracted he was by thoughts of Gillie.

"She's been on your mind nearly nonstop since Wednesday night," he told his reflection in the mirror as he finished tucking his shirt into his slacks.

Okay, so he liked the lady. She really was unique, had her own style and didn't take on airs.

What most people who wanted to stand out in a crowd adopted affectations to accomplish, she had naturally.

And in the past three days he had repeatedly had the feeling that he'd found a hidden treasure.

"Just take it easy," he told himself as he patted on after-shave, recognizing the urge to rush in and stake a claim. After all, he wasn't a kid anymore and he knew better than anyone how steep was the price of mistakes in one's personal life.

With his dressing finished, Kurt sat on the edge of his bed and picked up the phone on the night table. As he dialed the Connecticut number he wondered if he would actually get to talk to April. Half the time Carol wouldn't put her on the phone. And when she did he would spend the few minutes he was allotted saying, "April? Are you still there, honey?" into the silence at the other end. He felt frustrated just knowing what was coming. The art teacher brought his three-year-old to school on Friday, and the little boy had barely taken a breath while chattering to anyone who would listen to him. If only April were that outgoing...

"Hi, Carol, it's me," Kurt said when the call was answered by his ex-wife. The long silence that followed let him know that this was not going to be one of the times he got to talk to his daughter.

When she finally did speak, it was preceded with a disgusted sigh. "April can't talk. She has a cold."

Kurt closed his eyes and prayed for patience. "A cold isn't debilitating enough to keep her from a short phone call."

"It isn't that she's debilitated," Carol said scornfully. "It's that you upset her and I don't want her upset when she already doesn't feel well. But since you called anyway, I have some things to say to you."

"Let me talk to April for two minutes and then you can say whatever you want," he said in the firm, reasonable tone of voice he used on rebellious teenagers.

"I told you she can't talk to you tonight. Why didn't you answer my letter?"

He knew it was prudent not to tell her that he hadn't even read it. "I gave you my answer when you told me what you wanted. I will not give up my visits with April."

"They aren't visits, they're just times of torture for her."

"I'm her father and I have the right to see her," Kurt ground out.

"A father is someone who shares her life, who's there for her when she falls down or wakes up with nightmares or has a cold. It's Stuart who does all of that. It's Stuart who reads her bedtime stories and tucks her in. It's Stuart who's the father in her life."

Carol was good, Kurt had to give her that. She knew just where to put the knife and how to twist it. Not being a part of April's life was a bitter pill to swallow. In fact there had been times in the past two and a half years when he had been so hungry for a connection with her that he had even considered hiring a private detective to follow her at a distance and report back. He wanted to know what she did on a day-to-day basis, if she played with her friends or ate ice cream cones, or went to the park. "Your moving to Connecticut wasn't my choice. If you had stayed here so we could have shared custody I could have done those things."

"Our living in Connecticut is a fact of life and you might as well accept it and bow out gracefully. I know that you'd never give her up for adoption to Stuart and I don't have any grounds for forcing you to, or believe me, I would. But April will never think of you as her father anyway, so why continue to come where you aren't wanted and traumatize the poor child?"

"Because she's still my daughter," Kurt said tightly. "And maybe without your hostile hovering—"

"Hostile hovering?" Carol cut in, outraged.

"Yes, hostile hovering. Maybe if April and I spent a little time alone together without the antagonism she must sense from you, she'd relax and we could get to know each other. Then I wouldn't be one of the strangers she's afraid of."

Carol shouted, "How can I leave her alone with you when she cries and clings to me? If you really loved her you wouldn't condemn her to answering the demands of some long-distance parent she's never known."

"She's my child as much as yours, Carol, and I love her as much. It's no more right for me to be kept from having a relationship with her than it would be for you."

"Your tone sounds like a threat. Don't you even think about suing me for custody."

Kurt took a deep breath and tried hard to hang on to the thread of his patience. If he had any reason at all to consider Carol unfit, suing for custody was something he wouldn't hesitate to do. But he didn't have grounds. In every area besides this fostering of April's fear, Carol was a good mother. If anything, from the reading he'd been doing, he was more aware than ever of the importance of a mother's influence on the early development of a child.

He tried reasoning with her. "Of course I'm not threatening to sue for custody. All I want is a little time with her, for crying out loud. I just want to build my own relationship with her, can't you understand that? The kind of relationship she and I *should* have."

But as usual what he said didn't get through to his ex-wife. Her voice was loud and abrasive. "What I understand is that she's afraid of you. That not only is your coming here a nuisance but that it's cruel to put April through it."

The phone slammed in his ear.

Kurt hung up, leaned his elbow on the nightstand and rubbed his forehead. "Why the hell does it have to be like this?" he asked himself.

Every time he turned around he heard complaints about ex-husbands who didn't want to be bothered with the kids they had left behind. Look at Elijah, for instance. He had to have a stranger stepping into the job his father should be doing and, for a reason Kurt had yet to learn, apparently wasn't. And yet Kurt, wanting as much to do with his own daughter as he could possibly have, had to fight tooth and nail to see her or even to talk to her on the phone. There was no logic to the world.

But there was Gillie Hunter and the thought of their date put him back on his feet, if not back in high spirits.

It was probably unfair to inflict himself on her tonight, he usually wasn't great company after a run-in with Carol. And yet, feeling the way he did, there was something all the more appealing about seeing Gillie. After an encounter with his ex-wife, the hothouse flower, Gillie seemed like a breath of fresh air. Like just what he needed.

Gillie's doorbell rang at precisely seven. She was dressed in her gray slacks, black vest and white tuxedo blouse, but she had made a compromise. She'd tied a scarf around her throat and left the top button of her shirt unfastened.

Kurt approved because when she answered the door he smiled appreciatively and said in that deep voice of his, "Very nice."

Not bad yourself, was the first thing to pop into her mind as she let him in. He was dressed in tan corduroy slacks, a cocoa-brown V-necked sweater over a button-down shirt, and a tweed jacket. But all she said was, "Thank you."

As he had Wednesday night, he waited for her to precede him into the living room. Gillie appreciated good manners and so far his seemed impeccable. It would make him a good influence on Elijah.

"Where's our boy?" he asked after glancing around the room. "I brought him the *Sports Illustrated* issue I promised the other night."

The clean, woodsy scent of his after-shave wafted to Gillie as her eyes wandered up to his broad shoulders and the clean-cut line of his hair against his nape. She felt a little short of breath and consciously inhaled.

"He's staying next door with the Baumgardners tonight. T-bone steaks and a whole evening of uninterrupted video games supersede even *Sports Illustrated*—unless it's the swimsuit issue."

Kurt smiled that one-sided smile of his. "He tried to con me out of that one but I doubted you would approve."

"You were right. He spends so much time with the Baumgardner twins that he tends to think he's on the cusp of eighteen the same as they are."

"I noticed that." He also seemed to be noticing her all over again as his eyes scanned her from top to bottom to top again. "You really do look nice. I made reservations at the Old Neighborhood. Bob told me it was one of your favorite places."

She was flattered that he had gone to the trouble to find out. "Bob was right."

"I ordered a special bottle of wine when I made the reservation. It should be chilled and waiting for us right about—" he pushed up his sleeve to look at a dime-thin black watch "—now."

Finding out what her favorite restaurant was and preordering special wine made it hard for Gillie to keep this just-getting-to-know-Elijah's-friend dinner from getting too near to date-land. She told herself she shouldn't be enjoying his attention so much, so she tried to stop. Then he helped her on with her blazer and his after-shave wafted around her again.

So much for not enjoying.

It was not only very nice to be thought of and treated specially, but it put the mother part of her in remission, something this man had a particular knack for.

Gillie headed for the door as if she had to get there right that minute. "We'd better not keep your wine waiting."

The restaurant was only about ten minutes from Gillie's house and that time was taken up with directions. Decorated in antiques, Old Neighborhood had a cozy atmosphere. They were seated immediately in two high-backed wing chairs at a table beside an ornately mantled fireplace with a roaring blaze. Their waiter poured the wine as soon as they sat down and waited for Kurt's approval. When he gave it, both glasses were filled.

With Kurt watching to see if she liked it, Gillie tasted the light rosé. She didn't drink enough or know enough to tell the difference between this and any other wine but since it truly did taste good, she told him so. Then she tried to think of something the instructor in the How Singles Connect seminar had taught about starting a conversation.

"So, what was the high point of your week?" she said when she remembered.

"Meeting you and Elijah," he answered without having to think about it.

That embarrassed her. "Elijah seems fond of you already," she said, looking at her glass rather than at Kurt.

"I'm glad." He settled back with his wine and when Gillie glanced up, she saw that he seemed to be studying her. "Tell me about yourself."

She shrugged. "That would be a boring story."

"Oh, good, that's my favorite kind," he teased, not letting her off the hook.

She decided that telling about herself would give her the perfect segue to asking for the same from him, so she complied. "I was born and raised in California. My sister is twelve years older than I am so I always felt like an only child. I went to a small college no one has ever heard of and then I moved to Colorado, got married, had Elijah, got divorced and here I am."

"In a nutshell. How long were you married?"

"Five years."

"And you've been divorced five years."

"Roughly," she said. Feeling a familiar discomfort, she seized the moment to turn the conversation in the direction she wanted it to go. "Now you tell me about yourself."

"I was born in Oregon and raised in Utah by my mother after my father died when I was three. I went to UCLA for my bachelor's degree and liked it so well I stayed on for the rest of my education. Got married in my junior year, didn't have April until three years ago, got divorced and here I am."

Give a nutshell version get a nutshell version, she thought. "Your daughter is only three?" She had imagined her much older.

"Actually she's not even that for another couple of weeks. My ex-wife wasn't enthusiastic about starting a family. April was...an accident."

"You were divorced when she was just a baby, then."

"Mmm."

There was that reluctance again. Why? she wondered. "Are you close to her? I know she lives in Connecticut, but emotionally close?"

His expression seemed shadowed with what Gillie thought was sadness. "No," he said after a moment. "I'd give my right arm to say we are, but it just isn't true. In fact her mother would rather I didn't see her at all."

"Why is that?"

"I'm the skeleton in Carol's closet," he said disparagingly. Then he went on to explain the situation, painting a verbal picture of his ex-wife's pretentious bent and how his existence tarnished the image she had built for herself.

"So it's really just your ex-wife's hang-up and doesn't have anything to do with you as a father?"

Kurt's smile was lazy. "No. If it had anything to do with me as a father and Carol could legally keep me away, she wouldn't hesitate. But as it is she has no grounds."

His tone was sincere and Gillie didn't doubt him. It struck her as admirable that he would persist against such odds when another man might consider himself off the hook, free to go about his bachelor life. But rather than not say any more about it, her curiosity got the better of her. "I take it yours was not a nice divorce."

His response was a wry chuckle. "Divorce and nice are a contradiction in terms from my experience. How about yours?"

Gillie shrugged. "I guess nice isn't quite the right word. Maybe amiable is better."

"Was yours amiable?"

She thought about that. "I don't know what you'd call mine, actually. It certainly wasn't pleasant. And it hurt the way they all do, but the divorce itself was . . . a relief."

"The marriage was that bad?"

Again Gillie shrugged, feeling the same wave of helplessness she had at the time. "Phil was a marine in Vietnam. He suffered from delayed stress and the only relief he could find when it struck came out of bottles—liquor and pill bottles. It—" she cleared her throat "—it was something he hid from me before we were married. Afterward he couldn't conceal what was torturing him anymore. It wasn't a pretty way to live, but then having him disappear for months at a time was almost as bad." She watched her finger trace the rim of her wineglass. "Divorce got to be the only option when he wouldn't deal with his problems any other way."

"I'm sorry. It sounds like a nightmare."

Gillie swallowed with difficulty and shook off the ugly memories. "I don't think about it much anymore. It brings up bad feelings and they're like stray cats—feed them with poor-me thoughts and they're yours for life. I learned that if you let them wander out the way they wandered in you're better off."

"Good analogy," he said sincerely. "And you're right. I came to about the same conclusion when my divorce was finalized. You really do have to let go of the anger or it eats you alive."

Gillie wanted badly to ask some specifics about that anger but before she could he went on.

"Is that why Elijah hasn't seen his father since the divorce? Because of the pills and drinking?"

Gillie shrugged. "He hasn't seen him because after the divorce Phil never came back."

"You mean he's out of state?"

"I don't know. That's possible. His family is in Virginia, maybe he went there. He never contacted us after that."

Just then the waiter came to take their order. After he was gone, Kurt said, "I really didn't intend to take you out to dinner tonight and get into all this grim stuff."

"That's okay, I don't mind." The truth was that she was glad for the insight into his character. How he felt about his daughter and all the adversity he was willing to face because of her, told Gillie more about the man than any questions she could have devised. It struck her that it hadn't taken her long to go from a mother's natural caution of a stranger involved with her son to a woman who couldn't help being impressed by this man.

"So tell me," he said, still studying her. "What else do you like to do besides come to the Old Neighborhood for dinner? Avant-garde movies? Political discussion groups over espresso in the loft above a dusty old book store?"

Gillie made a face at both suggestions before realizing that they were probably things he liked to do and that was why he had brought them up. "No, that's not me," she said a little under her breath, not wanting to compound the insult. "I'm afraid I'm macaroni and cheese in a blackened redfish world."

He laughed. "What exactly does that mean?"

"That I'm a pretty simple, old-fashioned person who lives an untrendy life and who doesn't have much time for the things that are popular now. I usually have to choose sleep over entertainment, enlightenment and self-exploration."

One of his eyebrows rose. "That's probably for the best. I was always told self-exploration made you go blind."

Gillie smiled. It was very hard not to like this man. "I guess that explains my twenty-twenty vision."

Their conversation was interrupted by the arrival of dinner. When everything was served and they were left alone again he repeated his question, only now his tone was intimate. "So what do you do for entertainment?"

"You mean if I had entertainment worked into my budget?"

"No. I mean on what's allotted for it in mine."

She chose not to comment on that and just answer the question in general. "I like movies—the more lighthearted the better—walks, drives in the mountains, regular things. And of course, dining out. Cooking is not the love of my life."

Gillie didn't understand why that seemed to please him so much. "So lighthearted movies, walks, drives in the mountains and eating out are the macaroni and cheese, and avant-garde films or discussions in musty book stores are the blackened redfish?"

"Something like that."

"Then that makes me macaroni and cheese, too. Now tell me you also love to ski."

"Not this kid. The only slope I slide down is my driveway."

"But you're a fanatic for football."

"Not even if they played it in their underwear."

"That might be interesting. Tennis, basketball, hiking, camping?"

"Anything that makes people sweat should be banned from all civilized cultures."

"And I thought we were made for each other. Where do you stand on Mexican food, plays, museums, art galleries, Oktoberfest, window-shopping, concerts—"

"And chocolate-tasting festivals? Those are more my speed."

"Not quite a perfect match, but definitely workable." His grin was crooked again and Gillie was glad when the waiter came over to ask if everything was all right. Her pulse was too rapid and the flames from the fire beside their table seemed to have gotten hotter.

After they had finished their meal and Kurt had paid the bill, he pulled her chair out and reached a hand to her arm. The touch turned her blood to hot lava and Gillie actually had the sensation of that thick, molten stuff slowly working its way all through her body. All she could think of was that she had gone through this entire dinner without finding one flaw in this man. Worse than that, she had actually found even more reasons to like him.

Gillie almost didn't notice the lack of conversation on the way home, so lost was she in her own thoughts about whether or not to invite him in. On past dates this decision had been cut and dried. By now she was dying to escape into her own house, lock the door behind her and never see the man again. This evening seemed too short. That raised red flags in her mind and made her resolve to act as usual. When he walked her to her door she made it clear the "date" was over. "Thank you for dinner. I really did enjoy it."

"I'd like to see you again."

"We'll be seeing each other when you come for Elijah," Gillie hedged.

"We sure will," he agreed, undiscouraged. He leaned close to her. "But I meant that I wanted to see you again like tonight. Over and above the time I spend with Elijah."

Panic struck inside Gillie and she didn't know what to do. She wanted to see him again. And she didn't. "I don't think that's such a good idea. The whole point of this arrangement is for Elijah to have someone who concentrates solely on him. If he felt that we were sharing you it might defeat the purpose."

Gillie watched Kurt bite his bottom lip thoughtfully and nod his head again. "I can understand that, but I think we could work it out. I . . . like you, Gillie. I want to get to know you, to see more of you."

Her mind kept going back and forth, making itself up one way and then the other. She wanted to see him again and she could and she should, she decided on the one hand. On the other hand, she didn't want to see him on a personal level. He seemed too perfect. Twice before she had thought things and people were perfect, and she had learned the hard way not to believe that again. The only way to protect herself from that disappointment and potential devastation was to nip it in the bud.

She looked up at Kurt's face, hating that this decision was so hard to make. But before she could say anything he touched her lips with his, at first very softly, very gently, barely at all. His mouth was as cool as the night air and yet it sent that same hot lava through her veins again. Gillie knew she should cut this short, but as if her body didn't care what she thought, her head went farther back, accommodating the kiss, and her own lips answered his by parting just slightly.

The goodnight kiss went into something more. Kurt's lips opened to cover hers. His after-shave reminded Gillie of the mountains and he tasted of the peppermint he had had after dinner. She didn't realize she was lifting her hand to his chest until it was there, pressing against the softness of his sweater and feeling the hard muscles underneath. Oh, how she wanted to feel his arms tightly around her, pulling her to him, holding her....

But then the argument against it all gained some ground in her thoughts and Gillie broke off the kiss and stepped back. "I don't think it would be a good idea.... The best thing for Elijah... for us to go anywhere with this..." She was fumbling for words and not choosing any of the right ones. But it was the best she could do under the circumstances.

"I think you're wrong," he said, his deep voice low and rough, announcing the effects the kiss had had on him.

Gillie forcefully shook her head. She could feel his eyes boring into hers but she refused to look at him, knowing her willpower was not strong at that moment. When she didn't rescind her words, Kurt sighed heavily.

"It has to be up to you, Gillie. He's your son and whatever you think is best for him is what I'll do. But I don't agree that for us to see each other would somehow slight him and I wish you'd think about it."

Then he was gone, the sound of his heels echoing on the cement walk that led to the driveway.

Gillie couldn't get her fingers to fit her key into the lock. When she finally managed, she heard Kurt's car door close and his engine start up.

She had done what was best, she told herself as she stepped inside the house. Not only for Elijah, but also for her. Nothing and no one was ever exactly what they seemed. She just needed to remember that.

Chapter Four

It's six-o-six in the p.m. as we take this Tuesday into the night," quipped the disc jockey on the radio beside Gillie's drawing table.

She sat on a barstool, bent over a large piece of heavy paper thumbtacked in each corner. No matter how she looked at it, a shock absorber did not make an interesting picture.

Since she had always liked working on faces and figures best, fashion layouts were her favorites. But with a son to raise, house payments and other bills to pay, she couldn't afford to be picky. Drawing a car part might not strike creative ecstasy in her heart—or any other kind of ecstasy for that matter—but it would pay this month's electric bill.

"So ignore the cramp in your hand, Gil, and get it over with. Waste this quiet time and you'll be sorry," she said aloud.

Elijah was spending the evening with Kurt, just the two of them cooking dinner at Kurt's apartment and then watching some television. Male bonding.

The cramp turned into a muscle spasm and Gillie dropped her pencil in pain. "Oh, damn, that hurts," she told Rik, who stared up at her with droopy, lazy golden retriever eyes.

When the cramp stopped, Gillie picked up her pencil, felt the pain threaten to come back and set it down. "Okay, I guess we could stop for dinner."

Fifteen minutes later she had a plate of scrambled eggs in front of her on the drawing table. She stared at her somewhat cartoonish rendering of the shock absorber while she ate.

"What did Lijah say they were having?" she asked Rik as if he would answer. She should know. He'd been talking about the bachelor dinner since he'd gotten home from the video arcade with Kurt on Sunday. Franks and beans, salad, rolls and chocolate-chip cookies for dessert. They were going to bake the cookies themselves. Gillie would like to see that one.

She wiggled her fingers to be sure the cramp was gone for good, then went back to work.

If the cookies came out edible Lijah would eat a dozen of them before they had even cooled. She envied her son being able to eat anything and everything he pleased.

Actually there were a lot of little things about which she was happy for his sake and envious for hers.

Sleeping late on Saturday and Sunday morning when
she had to get up and work. Never worrying about
turning a light off or leaving water running. Seeing
Kurt....

That's not the same thing, she told herself quickly
and sternly. She just wished she wasn't stuck working
for the third night in a row. There was nothing wrong
with wanting a little leisure time.

So how come she never felt this way when her son
went off with anyone else? Had she honestly wanted
to spend Sunday afternoon in the video arcade with
them? Of course not. Did she really want to go to
Kurt's apartment for franks and beans and television
tonight? Not really.

She had made the right decision about not dating
Kurt. She knew it. She just needed to keep reminding
herself of it.

After he had left Saturday night her resolve had
been strong. He was a complication she didn't need.
A risk she wasn't willing to take now that her life was
in order. Kurt was Elijah's friend, someone who was
good for her son and bad for her.

So when he had called Sunday morning she had let
Elijah do all the talking, giving her permission through
him. She had had her son watch for Kurt's car so he
could run out before Kurt had a chance to come up to
the house. And then, just before she knew they were
coming back, she had called Robin, told her she had
to run a movie back to the video rental store and asked
if she could leave a note on the door for Elijah to go
there until she got back. The fact that there had been
no movie to return, that she had peeked through the

living room curtains watching for them and then waited until fifteen minutes after Kurt had left to call for Elijah to come home seemed a reasonable thing to do to avoid temptation.

It was the coward's way, and she knew it. But for some reason she was just too susceptible to this man to come into contact with him and resist this draw she felt toward him.

So why, when she had managed not to see the man, hadn't these feelings calmed down? She had figured not seeing him for a few days would give her a grip on her attraction and then she'd be impervious to him. Instead the longer she went without seeing him the more she wanted to. The less valid her reasons against it seemed. The easier it was to forget why she was better off alone.

She would have to see him sometime. She couldn't keep hiding out. Not only would that be awkward but it would be hard to keep up. Maybe she should look at seeing Kurt as simply personal contact that needed to be made so that everyone involved in Elijah's life could touch base and compare notes. That was all.

So why did she feel more deprived than she ever had in her life?

"One more plate of beans and you're going to bust."

"No si-i-r," Elijah answered, drawing out the word as he bounced up from where he sat on the floor. "I can eat another one. I'm going to tell Mom that food tastes better when you eat in the living room on the coffee table."

Kurt laughed. "That's only true when you're used to sitting at a dinner table every night, take it from me," he said as the boy carried his plate into the kitchen. "Better save room for our cookies."

When Elijah came back, his dish was only half full. "Mom thought it was funny that we were going to bake cookies. I told her it wasn't so weird. Bruce and Danny took cooking class at school."

"Home Ec," Kurt supplied. "But we're going to cheat. Ours are frozen and all we have to do is bake them."

"Good," Elijah said. "'Cause Danny said theirs tasted like rocks and I really like chocolate-chip cookies."

"And beans and franks. But you didn't do so well with the salad."

The boy didn't look at Kurt when he said, "I'm not real big on salad."

"Especially when somebody puts too much vinegar on it."

Elijah's grin was ear to ear. "Yeah, especially then. I wonder who did that?"

"Don't look at me," Kurt feigned defensiveness even though they both knew it was his heavy hand that had made dressing sour enough to pickle cucumbers. "So, how'd you do on that math test?"

Elijah shrugged. "I only missed two."

"Hey, all right. Good job. Any homework tonight?"

"Nope. I did it before you picked me up. My mom made me."

Seeing that Elijah was finally finished eating Kurt took the plates and salad bowls into the kitchen. "How is your mom?"

The boy followed him with the remaining dishes. "Okay, I guess. I mean she's the same as always, the same as when you asked on Sunday. Why? Did you think she was sick or something?"

"No, she seemed fine last time I saw her. I just wondered. I really like your mom." Kurt watched for Elijah's reaction. The boy shrugged as if that meant nothing to him.

Kurt had been debating with himself since leaving Gillie Saturday night whether to pursue what he wanted from this end. He hadn't said anything on Sunday because he hadn't been sure it was the wisest tack. But in the past two days Gillie had been on his mind so much he was lucky to remember his own name. He had decided to chance it.

"Did it bother you that I saw your mom Saturday night?"

"Why would it bother me?" Elijah asked.

"Well, our friendship—yours and mine—is kind of special. I just wondered if you felt like my spending time with your mom was cutting in on that."

"You mean like if you two were having dates and stuff?"

"Yeah, that's what I mean."

"Would you and me stop doing stuff?"

"You and I," Kurt corrected. "No, we wouldn't stop doing stuff. Maybe sometimes the three of us could do things all together, but you and I would go on just the way we agreed and sometimes I'd see your mom alone—if she wanted to."

Elijah jumped up to sit on the counter. "Does she want to?"

"I don't know."

"But you want her to," the boy guessed slyly.

"Yes, I would like her to."

"Robin says it's good for Mom to do stuff for herself, like Saturday night."

"What do you think?"

Elijah made a face that said he hadn't really thought about it at all. "She was in a pretty good mood Saturday. Well, not in the morning when she was cleaning the closet and saying she didn't have anything to wear. But later she sure was. She was singing and everything."

"Do you think that was because she and I were going out?"

"Or because she got the closet cleaned."

Kurt laughed. "So would it bother you if we saw more of each other. Your mom and me, I mean?"

"Is this like you're asking me if it's okay if you take my mom on dates?"

Kurt smiled. "Watch your feet so I can open the dishwasher and get these things put away."

Elijah pulled his knees up to his chest.

As Kurt loaded the dishwasher he answered honestly. "That's about it. I'm not sure she wants to date me, but if you give me the okay I'd like to try to convince her to."

Again Elijah shrugged in the way that kids had that said they didn't understand why an adult was making such a big deal over nothing. "I don't care, it's okay with me. But I don't know if she'll go. Robin's always trying to make her do stuff like that and she hates it. She goes once, like Saturday night, and then she won't ever go again. She says it's not much better than a poke in the eye with a sharp stick, whatever that means."

Kurt couldn't suppress a grin at that. "Well, if I get her to agree to go out with me I'll try to make it a little better than that."

Gillie wasn't watching out the window and she didn't have apple pie waiting at eight that night when Kurt brought Elijah home. She had spent the evening reminding herself that this was no different than if Elijah was out with his teacher Mr. Norman, who was five feet tall, four feet wide, and whose glasses rode a wart on the tip of his red nose. No different at all.

Except for that sense of eager anticipation she was trying to ignore.

"A glutton for punishment, that's what you are," she'd told herself.

It was confirmed when, a moment later, the slam of car doors sent a surge of adrenaline through her and left her short of breath.

"Hi, Mom," Elijah called as he came in the front door.

Pretending to be engrossed in her work, Gillie didn't glance up when she said, "Hi, Lijah." Then, as if she had just finished what she was doing, she sat back on her stool, tossed her French-braided hair over her shoulder in a way she hoped seemed very carefree and looked at Kurt as if it was the most common occurrence in the world that a man who appeared if he'd walked off the cover of *Gentleman's Quarterly* was coming into her house and that her pulse was not racing because of it. "Hi," she greeted him simply.

He held up a small brown paper bag. "I come bearing gifts."

She sat up straighter on her stool and tried to ignore the increased speed of her pulse. She'd never been offered a gift by one of Elijah's teachers and that was the way she needed to think of him, she reminded herself. But just then, Elijah, barely suppressing laughter, looked back at Kurt, and Kurt winked at him.

One of Elijah's pranks, Gillie thought. Her posture relaxed and something she didn't want to call disappointment slowed her heartbeat.

"What is it?" she asked suspiciously.

One of Kurt's eyebrows arched as he handed her the bag. "See for yourself."

Gillie accepted it hesitantly, holding it away from her with only two fingers. Her glance stuck for a moment on Kurt. Tonight he wore a plain, zippered sweatshirt over jeans and he still looked wonderful.

Then she saw Elijah fidgeting and giggling. She knew enough to exercise caution. "There's a snake in here, right? Probably poor Mrs. Rumson's."

Kurt looked confused and asked Elijah, "Is your mother accustomed to getting snakes for presents?"

"Just open it, Mom," Elijah prodded instead of answering.

Gillie looked from one to the other, then said to Kurt, "I believed you were a responsible, reliable, level-headed person who could be trusted. You wouldn't be turning against me now, would you?"

His smile was charmingly sincere, his eyes sparkling with intimacy as he winked at her this time. "I would never turn against you," he said with an obvious double meaning. "And I wouldn't let anything bad happen to you, either. Just open the bag."

Gillie made a show of taking a deep breath to steel herself. She braced the bottom of the bag in one palm and opened it very carefully with her other hand. Glancing inside at the contents she said, "I don't know if this is better or worse than a snake."

"You like chocolate-chip cookies, Mom."

"We thought that since you baked pie for us last week it was only fair that we share our cookies with you tonight."

"Yes, but I know what I'm doing in the kitchen. Am I going to be able to eat these without breaking a tooth?"

"Try one," Kurt urged, cupping her hand in his where it braced the bottom of the bag and nudging it toward her.

Gillie pulled away just a little too quickly, then tried to cover it up by teasing them with a disbelieving tone of voice. "You guys baked these, huh?"

"Go on, taste," Kurt said.

She finally complied, barely taking a nibble. "They're good," she said, surprised. "And you guys actually mixed the dough and baked these yourselves? I'm impressed."

It was Elijah's giggle that gave it away.

"Actually," Kurt confessed, "we baked them from little frozen knobs of dough. But we did put them on the pan and in the oven ourselves."

"Ah, why'd you tell?" Elijah groaned. "She'd never have known."

Gillie made a face at her son. "I knew something was up. All right, enough of your jokes, kiddo. It's a school night and you're off to bed. Remember, no argument, that was our deal for getting to go to Kurt's for dinner."

"We got to eat off the coffee table in the living room," Elijah announced as if it was a great coup. "And he said if it was okay with you maybe we could do a bachelor's dinner once every week. Can we?"

"I guess that depends on how you keep your part of the bargain now."

Elijah took off for his bedroom at a gallop.

"Neat kid," Kurt said as they both watched him.

"Thank you, I think so, too. And thanks for the cookies." Gillie took them into the kitchen and set the bag on the table. "I borrowed coffee from Robin and dug out a pot I got at a garage sale. Would you like some?" This was for courtesy's sake, she told herself. If Elijah's teacher was visiting, she would offer him coffee, too.

Kurt didn't need to be asked twice. "I'd love a cup." He slipped off his sweatshirt, exposing a plain navy T-shirt that stretched tight enough over pectorals and biceps to prove his athletic reputation and set off little fireworks in Gillie's stomach. She plugged the coffeepot in and got herself a glass of water to douse the sparks.

"What was all that about Mrs. Rummy's snake?" he asked, pulling out a kitchen chair and sitting down as if he was an old friend.

Gillie sat across from him. "Not Mrs. Rummy, Mrs. Rumson," she corrected. "She's an old widow lady who lives behind us. She grows a big garden in the summer and every now and then she'll find a snake in it. For years when she'd see one she'd pay Danny or Brian to catch it and take it to the creek. This last summer the job passed on to Elijah. Five dollars for catching the snake and getting rid of it. Funny thing though, the next week she found another one. And Elijah made another five dollars. By the fourth week, the fourth snake, and the fourth five dollars.... When poor Mrs. Rumson was sure she had a nest of them somewhere, I got suspicious. Sure enough, on the side of the house I found the snake in a box. Elijah figured he'd hit on a good deal. He just dropped the snake over the fence about once a week and waited for Mrs. Rumson to come across it. Easy money."

Kurt laughed. "He doesn't miss a trick, does he? How did you handle that one?"

"I made him take the snake to the creek the way he was supposed to in the first place. Then I sent him to Mrs. Rumson to apologize, return the money and volunteer his services as snake catcher for free from here on."

Kurt grimaced. "Ooo. High price to pay for being an entrepreneur." Then his expression turned approving. "But I'll bet that's the last time he pulls that one."

The coffee was ready and Gillie went to pour it. "Do you take cream and sugar?"

"No, just black, thanks."

"Did he behave himself tonight?"

"He couldn't have been better. We had a great time."

When Gillie had set a steaming mug in front of him and sat down again, he said, "It didn't occur to me until I got home Saturday night that we hadn't talked about any kind of schedule for my seeing Elijah. Then not seeing you on Sunday it still didn't get set up, so I thought we might talk about it tonight."

"Sure," she agreed, a little embarrassed, as if he were clairvoyant and knew about all her machinations to avoid him on Sunday.

"Do you have a preference?"

"It's really up to you. I appreciate that you're doing this and I certainly wouldn't feel right dictating terms. I can adjust to whatever works for you."

"You don't mind if we do a bachelor's dinner one night a week, then?"

Gillie shook her head. "Not as long as he's back by bedtime."

"No problem. And I want to spend at least one day of the weekend with him, too. Shall we leave that flexible or would you rather set something up formally?"

"We can decide it from week to week depending on what comes up for you."

Silence fell between them. Kurt sipped his coffee. Gillie felt uncomfortable and tried to think of something else to say. Then she remembered his daughter. "Did you get through to your little girl Sunday?"

"Believe it or not I still haven't. I called Sunday and her mother said she was feeling better but napping so I couldn't talk to her. Yesterday when I tried again April was well enough to be at a birthday party so I still didn't get her. But at least I know her cold is on the way out."

Gillie shook her head. "I can't imagine being separated from Lijah and not even getting to talk to him."

"I try to look on the bright side. After three blocks I'm assured of talking to her the next time I call. Carol won't push it that far." There was a moment's pause before he said, "Bob was right, though. Being with Elijah takes the edge off. I really enjoy him. We had an interesting talk. Several of them actually."

Those green eyes of his were staring at her again and it unnerved Gillie. She straightened up the basket of straw flowers in the center of the table. "Did you?"

"I've been enlisted to persuade you that he really is big enough to fly by himself to spend Thanksgiving with his grandparents in California."

"The next thing you know he's going to have the mailman in on that one. My parents send us tickets to fly out every Thanksgiving. But this year I have a deadline on the Monday after. There's no way I can go, and knowing Lijah, if left to his own devices he'll hijack the plane."

"Oh, I don't know. From talking to him I think he has a pretty good grasp of the line between mischief and maleficence. I doubt that you have to worry that he'll cross it. He also has a healthy sense of caution. I think you can trust him to behave himself in a situation like that. And I understand the flight attendants keep a close eye on kids traveling alone.''

Gillie couldn't suppress a slight chuckle. "So how much is his paying you to be his representative?''

Kurt smiled and took another sip of his coffee, his gaze staying on her over the mug. "He paid me in consent.''

"Consent? I don't understand.''

"He didn't really know he was paying me back. We discussed the Thanksgiving trip first. Then we discussed you and me.'' He let that hang in the air for a moment. "Have you thought any more about our seeing each other?''

Had she thought about anything else, would be a better question. Gillie took another drink of water. "I thought that was settled.'' She hated the hope that sprang to life in her at the thought that it wasn't, that he was going to pursue it.

"You said you thought it was bad for Elijah to have a sense of the two of you sharing me. So he and I discussed how he might feel if I were to date you, assuming of course that you agreed since you think it's not much better than a poke in the eye with a sharp stick.''

Gillie laughed uneasily at her words repeated to her. "He's a blabbermouth, that boy of mine.''

"He doesn't seem to have any problem with my seeing you both, separately or all three of us together.''

"You seem to have talked about this at some length."

"Not really. As a matter of fact he didn't seem to see a reason to discuss it at all."

For a moment Gillie was mesmerized by the sight of his long, thick index finger going round and round the rim of his coffee mug.

"So what do you say, Gillie? I promise to make it a lot better than a poke in the eye with a sharp stick. Or am I too late and that was how you considered Saturday night?"

"I didn't tell him that about Saturday night. It's just something I've said in the past in general," she answered too quickly. Why was it so important to make it clear to him that she hadn't said that about their date?

His expression seemed satisfied, as if she had agreed to something. "Good. Then how about this? I'll take Elijah with me to Arland's junior varsity football game Saturday morning, we'll spend the afternoon together, maybe take in a movie or something, and then you and I can have dinner that night."

Lord, but it was tempting. "I don't think—"

Just then Elijah charged into the kitchen, dressed in pajamas and a rubber monster mask. He was yowling and growling like a mad dog.

"Lijah," Gillie rebuked her son, even though she was actually grateful for the interruption.

Elijah slid his Halloween mask up to the top of his head and grinned at Kurt. "I told you it was a really scary face."

"You were right, too."

"Want to come and see my train set now? I have it all set up and ready to go." Anticipating her response, the boy turned to Gillie, "It'll just take a minute and then I'll go right to bed. I already brushed my teeth."

"Well, hurry up, then."

Elijah zoomed out the way he had come in. Before following, Kurt reached a hand to her shoulder, leaned over and said into her ear, "Think about it before you turn me down. We're both graduates of the romance school of hard knocks, but this isn't jumping in with both feet, this is just dipping your toe. And I have permission, so you don't have an excuse."

He left the kitchen and Gillie went to the sink for another glass of water. Alarms were shrieking in her head and she had an image of herself as Snow White being offered the poison apple, all red and shiny on the outside.

Just say no. Just say no.

The trouble was, she just didn't want to say no.

She drank another glass of water and wondered if she really had to refuse. Could she handle seeing him without getting in deep enough to be hurt?

Maybe like her worries about Elijah she was blowing this out of proportion, too. Out of all of the times she had worried herself sick thinking of what awful things *might* be happening to Elijah or *could* happen, nothing bad ever had. Maybe this was the same thing. A few dates, some time spent together didn't mean love, commitment, disappointment, pain. After all, the rest of her might-happens and could-happens never did.

Indulge yourself, a little voice urged.

Couldn't she sit on the lid of the attraction she felt for Kurt so it didn't suck her in, and splurge on some time of her own with him? Feelings didn't have to rule. She had had pain and an awful sense of failure and still made it through getting divorced. She had been tremendously aggravated and frustrated dealing with car salesmen and still bought the station wagon. She had been angry over the reassessment on her house that would have doubled her taxes and still managed to fight it down. Scared to death and worried sick over everything from Elijah's broken arm to a bout with bronchitis that had put him in the hospital, she had still managed to do what she needed to for him. Life was full of feelings that had to be ignored in order to function. So why couldn't the same willpower that had gotten her past those other feelings work for her now?

This was like the difference between renting an apartment and buying a house, she reasoned.

Rent an apartment and you could swim in the pool, work out in the gym, play in the recreation room. You could enjoy all the fun parts without any of the work. Buy a house and every nook, cranny, blade of grass and leaky pipe were your own problems. Dating was like renting an apartment. She wasn't buying into anything. When the paint began to peel she could walk away. And if Elijah wasn't disturbed by her seeing his big brother...

"You look like you're pondering nuclear war," Kurt said as he entered the kitchen and leaned against the counter beside her. The sound of his voice was a lure all its own. "Is it really all that serious a decision?"

It wasn't, she told herself firmly. She had just been acting as if it were. Gillie shrugged. "I sometimes have a tendency to make mountains out of molehills."

He poked a finger underneath her braid and slipped it behind her shoulder, leaving a trail of sparks everywhere he touched. "Let this one stay a molehill and say you'll go out with me," he said in tone both teasing and sexy.

"Elijah—" It was a sudden stab of doubt that uttered his name.

"Has already given his permission," Kurt finished, looking into her face. "And I will make absolutely sure that he isn't slighted in any way."

Gillie took a deep breath to clear her head. But the all too enticing scent of his after-shave only clouded it more. The man smelled good even when he wore his sweats.

Kurt rubbed the tip of her nose with one bent knuckle. "Come on, Gillie. Relax and let go a little," he beckoned.

"Nothing serious?" she tested, all the while hanging on to the edge of the sink as if it were a lifeline.

"Nothing serious," he confirmed with a pleased grin.

"I'm not interested in anything...serious..." she couldn't think of another word and then when she did she added, "or intense."

This time he drew his knuckle along the crest of her cheekbone. "Nothing serious or intense."

"I mean it," she said because it sounded as if he didn't. She let go of the sink and turned to face him, stepping away from him for effect.

He looked into her eyes, this time answering her sincerely, "I know you mean it. And I agree with you."

Gillie paused, as if she was risking her whole life. She swallowed. She doubted. But in the end she said, "All right, then."

He broke into a slow grin. "Good." He headed for the front door. Gillie followed. When his sweatshirt was back on, he turned to her, squeezing her arm with one of those big, powerful hands of his. "I won't make you sorry. That's a promise."

Watching him leave, Gillie just nodded and hoped it was the truth.

Chapter Five

The weather report on Friday night's ten o'clock news had warned that the light dusting of snow that had fallen all day would be twelve to fifteen inches deep by Saturday morning.

They had lied.

Gillie was sure there were at least twenty inches. And the snow was still falling.

"Oh, cool!" Elijah said, after he jumped up onto the couch to look out the front window.

"It's cool all right," Gillie agreed, grateful that she didn't have to worry about getting him to school for two days.

"Can I help shovel?"

Gillie knew that Elijah's help meant he would end

up kicking so much snow onto what she had already cleared that she would have to do it all twice.

"Sorry, kiddo. But you have to wait in the house and listen for the phone. You and Kurt were supposed to go to a football game today, remember? It'll be canceled and I'm sure the rest of your day with him will be, too, but he'll probably call to let you know for sure and if we're both outside we won't hear the phone ring." Thank heaven for small favors.

"Aw," Elijah groaned and slid down on the couch. Then he perked up. "But if he calls before you're done can I come out then?"

"You bet." Gillie had her fingers crossed.

"Can I invite him for snow food if we can't go anywhere?"

Snow food was one of the things that had become a small ritual over the years. Whenever they were snowed in like this Gillie made a pot of soup and baked bread. "I doubt if he would want to come out in this weather just for that, Lijah."

"But I could ask. He might."

"Snow food isn't really something to serve company."

"Ple-e-ease."

"I'm telling you he isn't going to want to come."

"Just let me ask him."

"Fine, if he calls, you ask him, but be prepared for him to say no. Anyone who goes out in this unless it's a dire necessity needs his head examined."

Gillie mixed the bread dough and set it to rise before dragging out her blizzard gear for the first time this year. When she hauled it all into the living room,

Elijah's interest switched from Saturday cartoons to his mother's snow shoveling preparations.

"Oh, boy, here we go," he snickered.

Gillie just smiled at him. She was used to being teased about this. Not only was it the winter delight of her son, but the entire Baumgardner family got in their share of entertainment value, too.

She already had on two pairs of knee socks. She stepped into chunky boots and stuffed the legs of her jeans in them. She put on a stocking cap, earmuffs and two mufflers. Over her turtleneck went a heavy cardigan sweater, buttoned to her throat, then a gray stadium coat, zipped to her chin. Completely swathed, with only her eyes peeking out, she pulled on a pair of gloves and then covered them with a pair of mittens.

By that point Elijah was rolling on the floor laughing, and Gillie spared him only a wave. She went into the garage for the snow shovel, then hit the button that opened the garage door. Standing with snow shovel at the ready, she stopped before she had even started.

There were tire tracks in her driveway.

She stared out at the two parallel lines that climbed her drive and then curved back onto the street. It was obvious that they had been made in the middle of the night.

There weren't any footprints in the snow, no sign that anyone had gotten out of the car. Somebody had probably just needed to turn around, she reasoned.

But why would someone pull into her sloped drive just to turn around when they could have used the flat one across the street?

An uneasy feeling crept over Gillie.

Then she shook her head. This was what she got for watching the news. It was why she rarely turned it on. Too many stories about muggers and murderers, and they put her so on edge.

Recovered from her fright, she plunged her shovel into the snow. She never glanced up from what she was doing, her mind wandering on its own.

Gillie jumped a foot at the sound of a car horn honking. She looked up to find Kurt's Volvo stopped in the center of the street. His window lowered with power-operated smoothness.

"Good grief. Is that you, Gillie?" he exclaimed.

What was he doing here? She nodded and waved rather than answer out loud.

"Move and let me pull up there," he called.

She stepped back into the garage as he gunned his engine to get a run up the hill.

"Kurt! Kurt!" It was Elijah's voice coming from behind Gillie.

She turned around to find her son hopping from one stockinged foot to the other on the frigid cement between the car and the house. She slipped her muffler down under her chin. "Elijah Phillip Hunter get inside right this minute. Don't you even poke your nose out in this cold without a coat."

"But Kurt's here," he said, as if that was reason enough.

"Now! Get in there!"

Elijah went up the steps into the doorway. "Hey, Kurt, do you need your head examined?" he called out.

"Uh, I don't think so," Kurt answered as he opened his car door.

"Mom said anybody who came out in this weather needed his head examined."

"Get inside, Elijah, and close the door," Gillie ordered ominously.

"Now you can have snow food with us," he said in a hurry before ducking inside and slamming the door.

"He's gone too far this time," Kurt said from behind her. "They'll put him in baby jail for mummifying his mother."

Gillie turned to find that handsome face grinning at her above a thick turtleneck the same sea green color of his eyes. "It's cold out here. Or haven't you noticed?" she answered back smartly.

"I noticed but I didn't think it was bad enough to turn a pretty lady into Nanook of the North."

His smile and the warm, teasing tone of his voice were charming, there was no denying it. But Gillie tried anyway. "How did you get here with the streets like this?"

"The main ones aren't too bad and the Volvo can get through just about anything."

"But why would you?" she asked bluntly. "Surely the football game was canceled."

"It was."

"You didn't have to come out in this mess just to tell us that. I assumed your day with Elijah was off, but a phone call would have done."

"The football game was canceled, not the whole day." He ducked his head inside the car. When he came out he had a brown paper grocery sack against his hip and three video cassettes in his hand. "I had dates with the two of you, as I recall. There's no way I'd let a little snow interfere with that, especially after what it took to get you to agree to see me, Ms. Hunter."

Gillie suppressed a smile ignited by a series of hot little sparks in her stomach.

Before she could say anything, he teased, "Besides, I had this itch to feel a snow shovel in my hands again."

"You *must* need your head examined."

"Well, if you'd rather do it yourself..." He eyed her up and down. "You're certainly dressed for it."

She looked from the leather bomber jacket that covered his sweater to tight jeans to his leather boots. "You're not," she decreed. "But I'm not dumb enough to turn you down no matter what."

The grocery sack rustled as he raised it slightly. "I'll go in and set this down and be right back. By the way, what is snow food?"

"Soup and fresh baked bread. It's what Lijah and I eat when we're snowed in, nothing fancy." She cleared her throat, realizing that she had no choice but to extend an invitation. "You're welcome to share it with us, though."

"Sounds good to me. I'll be right back," he repeated as he stepped around her and went into the house.

Gillie reminded herself to sit on the lid of these feelings that made the gray, winter weather suddenly seem cozy and wonderful.

By the time she had readjusted her muffler and was ready to start shoveling again Elijah bounded out of the house followed close behind by a loping Rik, with Kurt taking up the rear. As usual Elijah and the dog leaped into the nearest pile of already shoveled snow and caused an avalanche back onto the drive.

"Hey, sport," Kurt called to him as he took a second shovel from a peg on the garage wall, "play in the middle of the yard so you won't kick any of it back onto what's been cleared." Then he came out to where Gillie stood. He took her shovel and handed her his. "It's more efficient if I use the big one and you take the smaller."

She wasn't sure whether or not she liked his taking command, but she wasn't going to argue at the expense of lowering her muffler again.

His gaze devoured her once more, his head shook at the sight and his mouth stretched into a broad grin. "That getup really is amazing. I take it breathing the cold air bothers you?"

She could only nod.

"Why don't you go inside and let me do the rest of this, then?"

She shook her head. Maybe she was just being contrary, but this was her territory and she wasn't going to be summarily dismissed as if she couldn't handle it. Handling it had been too hard won.

"Okay. Then how about if you do the sidewalks and I'll finish the drive?"

This time she gave an exaggerated shrug and headed for the walkway that crossed to the front porch.

"It's been nice talking to you, Nanook," he called after her with a laugh.

Gillie just raised a mittened hand in acknowledgment.

With Kurt's help, the forty-five minute job was cut down to twenty. Both Elijah and Rik managed to cover themselves in snow and ice balls that clung to mittens and paws like thistles. Still, when Gillie next freed her mouth from her muffler and called them to come inside, Rik kept doing high jumps over snow drifts and Elijah moaned and groaned. He only conceded when Kurt promised they would go out again later to build a snowman.

When they were finally all in the house Elijah peeled off his winter gear in a matter of seconds and herded Rik downstairs to dry off. It didn't take Kurt much longer to slip out of his bomber jacket. Then he settled on the arm of a cream-colored recliner and watched Gillie.

"Thanks for the help," she said, clamping the tips of her mittens between her teeth and yanking.

"I was taught to work for my snow food."

Gloves followed mittens to a spot in front of the heat register and then she took off her coat. "What's in the bag you brought?"

Kurt crossed his arms over his chest, his gaze following the unwrapping of Gillie's head and neck from two mufflers, earmuffs and stocking cap. "Popcorn, pretzels, peanuts—the three basic movie-watching food groups—and a bottle of wine for sipping in front of a fire when the movies are over, Elijah's gone to bed and it's just you and I."

That thought brought a tightening to her insides. "If your feet are cold you ought to take off your boots," she advised in the tone of voice usually reserved for Elijah.

"I'm fine for now, thanks, Mom," he chided gently and then mused, "You know, if I had to bet on it, I'd say you slip into your mother routine with me whenever you're feeling the least like one. Guess I should count it as a compliment."

She'd been found out. She made a mental note never to do it again and changed the subject as if she hadn't heard him. "What movies did you bring?"

"Something about a dinosaur named Baby, another one about a bicycle race and *The Quiet Man* with John Wayne—my all-time favorite."

Gillie took off her sweater, the last of her gear.

"You aren't going to stop now, are you?" he asked in that sexy, insinuating timbre his voice sometimes took on.

It sent a skitter of goosebumps up her arms but Gillie ignored them and pretended offense. "I beg your pardon."

He shrugged. "You can't shoot a guy for trying. So tell me, do you have two sets of long johns under there, too?"

"None of your business," she told him loftily.

His gaze raked her up and down. "No, that would add about five pounds to the way you look and it's not there. You're still your svelte self."

The tingle and thrill his compliments caused were crazy, she told herself. But there they were anyway. "Last chance to put your boots next to the register," she offered because thrill or not, she didn't know what to say to him.

"No, thanks. Put yours there." Gillie could feel his gaze staying with her as she did. "It's no wonder you don't ski. If this is what you wear just to step outside of your house I can't imagine what it would take to keep you warm on a mountain slope."

"That's part of the reason I don't do it."

"And you'd be hard to beat at a game of strip poker afterward."

"Coffee?" she asked in a voice two octaves higher than usual.

"Actually a cup of your tea sounds good."

Gillie led the way into the kitchen. "Just let me knead the bread dough and I'll put it on."

"You have at your disposal one of the world's best bread dough kneaders. Use me."

Oh, the double meanings she was hearing! She had to stop it. "One of the world's best bread dough kneaders?" she repeated skeptically.

He lifted the towel that covered a bowl on the kitchen table and took a look inside. "That's right," he confirmed as he went to wash his hands as if he really did know what he was doing. "Baking bread was my mother's remedy for sad feelings. She used to say nobody could stay feeling bad with the smell of bread baking and a warm slice of it to look forward to."

Gillie handed him a paper towel to dry his hands. "I never thought about it like that, but I suppose it's true. I don't do it for sad times but it does give us something to look forward to when we're shut-ins." She hadn't made the correlation before, but he, like Elijah, had been an only son raised by a mother alone. It suddenly occurred to her that that was something to mine. "Did you miss having a father?" she asked as she filled the kettle, thinking of one of the things she always wondered about Elijah.

Kurt shrugged. "Of course. My mother was a terrific lady but there was a gap she couldn't fill."

She took down two cups, then sat at the table while he plunged into the dough. "Did anyone play big brother for you?"

"No. I suppose that's how I got to be such a jock. Being on football teams, baseball teams, basketball, all provided contact with surrogates in the form of coaches. But it was no replacement for the times when I just wanted to talk to a man about what was on my mind."

"Things you couldn't talk about to your mother?"

For a minute he stopped what he was doing and looked down at her. "Being a girl, weren't there *things* you didn't feel comfortable talking to your father about?"

"Well, sure, but a mother—"

"Is still a woman."

"You're a sexist," she accused because she didn't like to think there was anything Elijah couldn't talk to her about.

He smiled at her as if that didn't offend him in the slightest. "A boy needing to talk to a man about some things, my lovely wispy-haired lady, is a fact of life."

Gillie smoothed a palm over the feathery strands her stocking hat had loosened from her braid. "I told him the facts of life," she said defensively.

He raised his eyebrows at her. "Oh, I see. The facts of life being the only thing you figure a boy might feel uncomfortable talking to his mother about, or the only thing a man might have to teach. Careful, you're treading on sexist territory yourself. And you're wrong."

He went back to kneading the bread dough.

"What else, then?" she asked.

"Believe it or not, it takes a man to teach a boy to be what a woman wants."

"Assuming a woman wants a coarse, tough, macho man," she said snidely.

"Wrong, wrong, wrong."

His hands were very large, Gillie noticed, his fingers long and thick. "I beg your pardon," she repeated, though she wasn't affronted.

"It takes a man to teach a boy that it's all right—not sissy or weird—to be soft, sensitive, considerate, gentle. That it's okay to have feelings and to show them."

Those hands of his worked the dough in a way that seemed to illustrate just the kind of masculine gentleness he was talking about. Gillie fidgeted and forced her gaze up his long, muscular arms and broad shoulders to his face. It was suddenly difficult to swallow. "You don't think a woman can teach that?" she challenged because it felt safer.

"A woman can teach it but without a male role model to show it, to approve of it, a boy finds it suspect. From his peers he gets the we-all-have-to-be-tough-enough-to-chew-glass stuff that makes everything to do with Mom eventually synonymous with weakness. That needs tempering to find a middle ground or he ends up in one extreme or the other.''

''Are you telling me I've warped my son?''

''Not at all. What I'm telling you is that, for instance, he sits in on his older cousin's big-man swagger talk that makes a *real* man a carnivore and women raw meat. That's okay, it's normal, but the fact that at the same time Bruce and Danny are living with a man who loves his wife, respects her and treats her as an equal means there's a better than average chance the Baumgardner boys will come to grips with the macho part, integrate it with what they see in their father and turn out to be decent men. But Elijah is removed from Bob. He doesn't confide in Bob. He thinks that around Bob he should act like what he sees of Bruce and Danny, like a big tough guy. He misses the example that tempers it. I'm not in Elijah's life to teach him about sex, Gillie. I'm in it to teach him about being a man. Believe it or not, they're two separate issues.''

Somehow her gaze had slipped back down to his hands and suddenly she pictured them kneading her skin the way he was kneading that dough. It brought a world of sensations alive in her that she hadn't felt in years.

''I think we can have tea now,'' his voice interrupted her thoughts.

Gillie came up with a jolt when she realized the kettle had boiled over. Flustered, she charged to the stove and tried to think of something to say to cover her preoccupation. "Who taught you, then, if you didn't have a big brother?"

He came to the sink beside her to wash the dough off of his hands as Gillie poured water into the cups. "Some of it came out of bits and pieces, I guess. Watching the fathers of my friends, some of the men my mother dated. But more of it came later, when I was in college, taking psychology classes and getting more and more in touch with my softer side. Suddenly a childhood fantasy was becoming a deep desire and it seemed pretty unmacho. Believe it or not, it came to a head when I was ready to graduate with my bachelor's degree and I was deciding whether or not to play pro football. There was suddenly a clear choice—end my education there, play ball and continue on with the big man persona, or admit to the other side of me, the side that wanted to go on learning, that wanted to work with kids, to nurture and teach. It was quite a struggle, believe me. I'd like it if I could spare Elijah that."

Being with this man was like riding an emotional roller coaster. One minute she was overcome with the elemental sensual feelings of a woman and the next he had deeply touched her as a mother and roused gratitude that this kind of man was taking her son under his wing. "What was your childhood fantasy that turned into a deep desire?" she asked him softly.

He turned to face her. "I loved my mother," he said matter-of-factly. "But just the two of us didn't seem like a family to me. And I wanted that more than anything. I used to lie in bed at night and wish that whichever man she was seeing would marry her and they'd have kids. But it never happened. When I hit the last year of college I began to realize that as an adult I could have what I'd wanted so much and missed as a kid. I'd be the parent instead of one of the children. I'd have a family of my own. In a clique with the man-as-carnivore, woman-as-raw-meat mentality, prodigious conquest meant masculinity. Getting married and having kids meant stupidity to say the least, and certainly something a lot less than macho. As it was put to me, why would I willingly give up being a superstar stud with a horde of football groupies hot on my trail unless there was something wrong with my hormones?''

The laugh that followed made it clear the question hadn't threatened him. Gillie could only wonder at how anyone could question this man's hormones. It seemed overwhelmingly obvious that they were all alive and in perfect working order.

''I wonder if Elijah feels like we're not a real family and fantasizes about having one?'' she said more to herself than to him.

Kurt leaned his forearm on her shoulder and turned her face to his with a single finger under her chin. ''What are you going to do about it if he does? Go out and rent him one?''

That's what she was doing with Kurt, she thought, and suddenly felt guilty. He was so conscientious. He had thought a great deal about the role he needed to play in Elijah's life and was obviously taking it very seriously. And all the while she was thinking of him just as a rental, something to use temporarily.

But regardless of how conscientious he seemed, or how seriously he seemed to take his role in Elijah's life, she knew better than anyone that things and people were almost never what they seemed. And besides, Elijah was really only a rental to him, too. A stand-in to fulfill his frustrated paternal instincts. Remembering that made her feel better.

"Do you think life-size, blow-up dolls would work?" she said finally. "I could get him some for Christmas."

"Perfect."

His mouth puckered slightly, as if he was on the verge of kissing her, and he had leaned over near enough to make it seem like an imminent possibility. Back to pure, elemental, sensual feelings.

Gillie took a deep breath to cool them and said in a hurry, "I'd better get the soup on or we won't have any dinner."

One side of his mouth lifted in a slow, knowing smile. "And I promised our boy a snowman. I have every intention of tiring him out so he falls asleep early tonight."

"Good luck," Gillie returned dubiously. "*Our boy* has the energy of three kids and a hyperactive gerbil."

"He's still no match for a one hundred and eighty-five pound man who can't wait to get his mother alone." He did kiss her then, not too short, not too long, as if he was giving her a little taste of things to come.

The snowman turned into a wall behind which Kurt and Elijah manned an all-out attack on Danny and Brian when the two teenagers came out to shovel their own walks. From the picture window in her living room Gillie watched the war. She didn't know when she'd seen her son as animated and carefree and it left her all the more convinced that her cousin-in-law's idea of a big brother was a good one, his choice of Kurt a stroke of genius.

Kurt's participation in the snowball fight never regressed to his behaving like one of the boys. Instead he acted as Elijah's backup, supplying ammunition and tactical advice that gave her son the upper hand over his cousins for once. Elijah's confidence seemed to grow right before her eyes and she realized that if there had been any doubt left before that this man might not be good for him, it had ended today.

It also occurred to her that a part of Kurt's appeal was his maturity. She hadn't thought about it before, but in the past five years the men she had met had seemed like adolescents in adult bodies. In fact, she thought that there had also been a certain childishness in the two men with whom she had been seriously involved.

But Kurt was different.

And she liked the difference. More than she wanted to admit.

They spent the afternoon watching the bicycle race movie, which only added fuel to the fire of Elijah's enthusiasm since he saw himself as the underdog in his dealings with his cousins and in the movie, the under-dog won out.

By the time the movie was over, the smells of baked bread and vegetable soup mingled. Elijah set the table while Kurt sliced the warm bread and Gillie ladled soup into bowls. The men took over kitchen clean-up when the meal was finished. Then the three settled in for the rest of Kurt's movie fare—with Elijah on his stomach in front of the fire, Gillie hugging the arm of the couch and Kurt close beside her. It was a good thing that between the dinosaur movie and *The Quiet Man* Gillie had her son put his pajamas on because sometime during the third feature he fell asleep on the floor.

"Shall I carry him to bed?" Kurt whispered when the movie was over.

Gillie shook her head. "He'll wake up and get mad for being treated like a baby."

"Then how about if you get him tucked away for the night and I pour the wine?"

The relaxed state Gillie had settled into as the day and evening had progressed suddenly became something else. But there was no turning back now. And she wasn't even sure she wanted to.

With Elijah barely aware that he had been moved into his bed, Gillie went back to the living room. She found Kurt tending to the fire; two glasses of chablis were waiting on the coffee table.

She really did feel like a teenager, she thought. But it wasn't an altogether bad feeling. It was also not an altogether bad feeling to have had another adult in the house all day lending a hand. In fact, between not having to clean the dinner mess and sitting back on the couch while he took care of the fire, she was beginning to feel pampered.

"Well, you were wrong," Kurt informed her as he closed the firescreen. He picked up the wineglasses and sat beside her on the sofa.

Gillie accepted one of the glasses and tried not to think about how his thigh was pressed against hers. "What was I wrong about?"

"Our boy has the energy of four kids and two hyperactive gerbils. It must be tough being a single parent, doing everything yourself." He put his arm around her as easily as if he had been doing it for years. The answering flutter of Gillie's stomach was the only evidence against that.

"Mmm," she agreed. "It's not something I would have chosen. But we get by."

"I see a lot of single parenting. Too much. And I admire the stamina it must take."

Gillie laughed. "Stamina is a good word. But we all do what we have to." She looked over at the fire. "It's hard not having a sounding board, though. I worry a lot about whether or not I'm doing things right. Am I too strict? Am I too lenient? Did I come down too hard on him or not hard enough? Without someone else around to say: back off, it's not such a big deal, or you're right, this time he's really out of line, I'm never too sure."

"But you didn't remarry."

It was a leading statement that Gillie chose to joke her way out of. "Sure I have. Six times. I just don't like to spread it around." She could feel his eyes on her and turned her head to see why. But there was no clue in his expression.

Then he smiled, slowly, lazily. "It's hard to believe someone hasn't grabbed you up."

"Oh, I stay away from the grabbers. How about you? I always figured it was easy for a man to have just about everything he wants in the single's world. Any time. Any way. Anywhere."

"I guess that depends on what he wants. Me, I'm discriminating."

"Discrimination is illegal."

"Not this kind."

Gillie took a sip of wine only to find it was nearly gone. He took her glass and set it on the table next to his.

"I've been waiting a week for this," he told her in a voice that was deep, husky and barely audible.

With his palm against her cheek he turned her face up to his, smiled again in that lopsided way of his, then lowered his lips to hers. There was nothing tentative in this kiss, nothing questioning or hesitant. His mouth was warm and moist, gently insistent.

Gillie was surprisingly relaxed, as if her tension had been caused more by the anticipation of what might happen between them than in it actually happening. His lips parted over hers and she found in herself a willingness to match him. She didn't want to think about anything more than how good his kiss felt.

His arms closed tight around her and she realized she had been longing for this all week. She slid her arms under his and pressed her palms flat against the hard expanse of his back.

The tip of his tongue ran lightly along her upper lip and sent tingling sensations through her. Little by little every sense was becoming heightened, every nerve was awakening to feelings she had long ago forgotten. Wonderful feelings. And when his tongue found its way into her mouth, she met it with her own, welcomed it, savored it.

His kiss deepened, grew hungrier, more urgent. He cupped the back of her head and Gillie arched back to accommodate him. The fluttering inside of her was rapidly turning to more demanding cravings, bringing to life her nipples pressed against his chest and a tight cord that stretched to that spot between her legs that had been left sleeping for so long. And all this time she hadn't thought she missed these feelings. She had thought she could live without them.

She had been wrong.

Needing to feel more than his sweater, she reached up to the back of his head, finding her way to his nape. His skin was so warm, so alive. She was so alive.

His mouth was opened wide and so was hers. His face was rough against the softness of her skin, his hands were holding her as tightly as hers were him. She couldn't breath, she didn't need to. But what she did need. . . .

Gillie stopped.

She opened her eyes, drew away from his kiss and dropped her glance down until she was staring into his Adam's apple. Her breathing was fast and shallow, her heart racing, and every inch of her body shrieked for more. But her mind had put on the brakes.

"Gillie?" Kurt asked in a voice both rough with passion and tender with confusion.

She shook her head. "And I thought only teenagers could get carried away. I can't do this. I don't...we haven't known each other that long...Elijah...."

For a moment he didn't say anything. Then he sighed a long breath as if he had been holding it. "I won't say I don't want you because it would be a lie."

Gillie heard him swallow and sensed him working to get control over himself. She straightened away from him and let her arms fall to her lap.

"There's powerful stuff at work here, lady," he said in that same husky tone.

"Too powerful."

"No such thing. But I won't do anything that sets this relationship off in the wrong direction." He tipped her face up to his. "Make no mistake about it, anything this good should go on." He smiled wanly. "Now shove me out the front door before the snow gives me a viable excuse not to go home tonight."

He took a deep breath and pushed himself to his feet. Gillie followed, forcing limbs that were still heavy with wanting. When he had put his coat on and zipped it up, he took her by the shoulders and looked down into her eyes.

"Powerful and special, Gillie. Something we should treat very carefully. Something we should nurture. Trust me."

He kissed her once more, a kiss only tinged with the passion that had bound them moments before, and left.

But she didn't trust him, she thought as she closed the door after him and fell back against it. And worse than that, she didn't trust herself.

"It's just need," she said aloud as if the sound of her own voice would make it true. Need that had been suppressed all this time and triggered by a particularly handsome, charming, intelligent, sensitive, kind, warm . . .

"Need," she repeated firmly to stop her thoughts. It didn't mean she was falling for the guy. It was just biological need born of abstinence. And now that she was aware of it, she could toss it in the pot along with the feelings and attraction and keep the lid on it all the way she had decided before.

At least she hoped she could.

Chapter Six

The wedding invitation had said something about Tom and his fiancée being so thankful for having met each other that they felt the most appropriate time to be married was during Thanksgiving.

But then every one of Tom's weddings had revolved around some romantic theme, Kurt thought as he served himself a cup of coffee from the food-laden buffet table.

He and Tom had been college roommates. They were good enough friends for Kurt to be his best man the first time around, that one had been on Valentine's Day. By the second marriage their friendship had been diluted by time and the demands of living their own lives, so wife number two's brother had been the witness for that Fourth of July ceremony. The third one was, Tom had sworn, a new beginning; hence the New Year's Day wedding. Kurt wondered which his swarthy old friend was going to run out of first—brides or holidays.

Kurt wandered toward a corner of the crowded apartment. He'd checked his watch and knew that about the time he finished this cup of coffee he could politely leave. After all, he had celebrated enough of Tom's weddings not to have to stay to the end of today's festivities, especially since he had festivities of his own to prepare for.

That was a good thought.

Gillie had relented and let Elijah fly to San Diego for Thanksgiving, which had opened the way for Kurt to insist she share the holiday with him. Only this time it hadn't taken a lot of insisting. A good sign. But then, so far, Kurt hadn't seen any bad signs in regards to Ms. Gillie Hunter.

"Came alone, huh, pal?" The groom's voice interrupted Kurt's thoughts.

Kurt smiled at his shorter friend. "Not by choice." He had asked Gillie to come but she was too swamped with work.

"Have you, uh, noticed the redhead in the white dress?" Tom poked an elbow into Kurt's ribs.

"You mean your bride? Very nice."

"Chuckle, chuckle. I'm talking about the one on the couch. Something, isn't she?"

She was. "Don't tell me you're lining up number five already."

"Not for me. For you,"

"Uh-oh," Kurt said, as if he really hadn't seen this coming a mile away.

Tom missed the sarcasm. "She's Heather's cousin."

"That's nice."

"Come on, I'll introduce you."

"Thanks, but no thanks."

"She's perfect for you."

"Too late. I've already found someone who's perfect for me." And Gillie was, too, he realized as he said it.

Tom arched pale eyebrows. "Oh-ho, tell me about this."

What should he say? That Gillie was sweet, a touch naive, another touch nutty, beautiful, bright, unpretentious? Or should he say she made him feel less jaded, showed him that there really did exist a woman who had old-fashioned values, who didn't have an angle or an agenda that was going to be met even if it meant bulldozing over other people to do it? Who made him feel good and comfortable and free to be himself, all the while his hands were itching to be all over her? No, he couldn't say any of that to Tom. So instead he settled for, "I've just met someone I care about."

"Is she gorgeous?"

Kurt looked at his friend's very young, buxom bride, her reddish hair as wild as a lion's mane, her nails long, her makeup too obvious, her lips outlined and gleaming. She could have walked off the pages of a fashion magazine. Then he took in the rest of the women in the room, all perfectly clothed, coiffed and cured. They all looked alike to him. Compared to them, Gillie was very down-home. The comparison made him smile.

"Yes, she's gorgeous to me."

"Built?"

"Just right."

"Rich?"

"Not by a long shot. And she has a little boy."

Tom groaned. "I always avoided the ones with kids. Take my advice and do likewise. They're only an added complication."

That brought an image of Elijah to mind. Kurt smiled again. "Actually, I like her son as much as I like her."

"I'll bet she has a draft horse for a dog and you even like it," Tom said snidely.

Kurt laughed. "As a matter of fact—"

"You've got it good, I can tell. When's the wedding?"

"We're talking about me, not you, remember?"

"Don't tell me you've sworn off for good after just one try?"

Kurt shrugged. "Not for good, no. I'm just not quite as impulsive as you are."

"Well, this is it for me, bucko." Tom waved to his new bride standing across the room.

"I hope so," Kurt said, meaning it. But he had heard this same thing from his friend three times before so he couldn't help feeling pessimistic. He checked his watch. "I'm going to have to take off. Congratulations, and give my best wishes to your bride."

"Thanks, and if things don't work out with the package deal give me a call. I'll set you up with Misty."

"I'll keep it in mind," Kurt lied on his way out. A month ago he might have taken Tom up on the offer. But not now. His friend's wedding had accomplished two things. It had reminded him of the kind of woman he had dated in the past and married, and illustrated just how different Gillie was from them all. It was a difference he liked. And being here had brought home to him just how much he did appreciate Gillie, how strong his feelings were for her.

Kurt thought that he had come away with a better understanding of his impulsive friend, also. It wasn't as if he had known Gillie all that long, and yet his own impulses were strong. In fact, they were fast becoming overwhelming.

It was noon on Thanksgiving Day and while concentrating on drawing the intricacies of a satin evening bag adorned with a velvet rose and a twisted cord shoulder strap, Gillie remembered the commotion that had awakened her the night before.

Shortly after midnight the wind had blown open the gate on her six-foot-high cedar fence—directly under the bedroom window of her cantankerous, complaining neighbor, Joe Morrison.

The bang and creaking hinges had roused her and Rik, setting the dog to barking like crazy. She had gotten up, peeked out of every window to make sure no one was trying to break in, then gone back to bed, swearing that if only the swaying gate would stop on its own she would replace the latch with something she could lock up tight enough for this never to happen again.

Now she stopped working and went around the garage to the gate.

"Great minds work alike."

Gillie jumped a foot at the sound of her cousin's voice from behind her.

"I was just coming to see about that midnight noisemaker of yours," Robin said.

"It even woke you guys up?" Gillie asked, making a face and glancing at the Morrisons' bedroom window.

"We hadn't gone to sleep yet. Bob was just about to get dressed and come over when it quit. You didn't—"

"Not me. I laid in bed and prayed for divine intervention to stop it."

"I figured," Robin said. She looked past Gillie at the gate, pointing with her chin. "Then how did it get latched?"

Gillie turned to find the hook not only through the loop but bent so it couldn't come free as easily.

Then Robin laughed knowingly and pointed to several shiny black drops on the cement. "I don't think there was anything divine about this intervention. It looks like the hinges have been oiled, too."

"Joe keep-the-neighborhood-as-quiet-as-a-mausoleum-Morrison," Gillie surmised. They both knew the man had complained a few weeks ago about Elijah's taking his bicycle out through the gate, claiming the creaking hinges disturbed his nap.

"I heard he and his wife were leaving yesterday morning to spend the holiday with their daughter, but they must have left this morning instead."

"It has to be either Joe Morrison or more of Elijah's elves."

"Huh?"

"When we came out one morning to find that Danny had raked our leaves, the first thing Lijah thought was that the job had been done by elves in the middle of the night while we slept."

"Danny raked your leaves?" Robin repeated, surprised.

Whoops. Not something she should have said, Gillie realized. "He did me a favor," Gillie said to cover up, then quickly changed the subject.

"Can't you just see old Morrison grumbling and griping his way out here in the middle of the night to bend the latch and oil the hinges?" Gillie blew a kiss to the bedroom window. "Thank you, Joe." Then to Robin she said, "Now if only I could find a way for my leaky faucet to disturb his sleep so he'd come and fix that, too." She rubbed her arms. "It's too cold to stand out here, let's go inside."

"Only for a minute," Robin said as she followed Gillie. "I know you're working and we have to leave for Bob's parents' house pretty soon." They had barely closed the door, "With Lijah gone, we weren't sure you were even here. Or that you were here alone. How are *things* going?"

Gillie fluffed the pillows on the couch. "*Things* are going fine. Lijah had a terrific time flying alone, my folks were there when he got off the plane and everything went smooth as butter. I'm right where I need to be to finish this assignment and hit my deadline."

"You know what I meant."

Gillie brushed lint from the recliner. "You didn't want to know if Lijah got in all right?" She played dumb, sitting down on the coffee table and casting an innocent gaze up at her cousin.

Robin sat beside her. "Of course I did. I also wanted to know if, since he's gone, you and Kurt seized the moment and—"

"I was home, in bed, all by my little old self."

"How boring. But you are still going to his apartment for dinner tonight, right?"

"You know I am."

"And then the two of you will have the whole three day weekend—"

"To work so I can meet my deadline."

"All work and no play—"

"Pays the bills."

Robin sighed and gave in. "You do like him, though, don't you, Gil? I mean you must since this is the first time in five years that you've had more than one date with anybody and it seems like every time I look out my window his car is here."

"He's a nice man. And he hasn't been here all that much."

"That's it? Just, he's a nice man?"

"Uh-huh. That's it." Oh, you liar you, she scolded herself.

Robin stood and went back to the door. "If you had a man here last night Mausoleum Morrison wouldn't have had to fix your gate and you wouldn't be in line for the dressing down you'll get when he comes back.''

"Mmm," Gillie agreed.

"You don't fool me, Gillian Hunter. I know that no matter how unaffected you want to appear, you think it would have been nice to have had Kurt there to hold you and get your mind on something that's fun."

"You think you know me so well," she said non-committally.

"Yep, I do." Robin left with her nose in the air.

Okay, so she was right.

After a call to Elijah and her parents to wish them all a happy Thanksgiving, Gillie took a bath, washed her hair and ironed her new blouse. The price of two and two-thirds pizzas, that was what this blouse had cost. But the drawback of seeing a man more than once was that you couldn't wear the same clothes every time.

"And I was due for a new blouse," she rationalized as she pressed the red crepe confection that wrapped around in front and allowed her to create as deep or as shallow a V-neckline as she wanted. She wasn't feeling like herself and there was a part of her that wondered just how daring this other person would let that neckline be.

Was it because she was separated from Elijah for the first time since he had been born? Or was it the anticipation of an evening with Kurt?

She honestly didn't know. Maybe both. But it was as if Gillian Hunter, ever-practical mother, was asleep somewhere inside of her and Gillie Hanrahan, carefree starry-eyed teenage girl, had taken over.

"Oh, good, so now on top of being an overly imaginative paranoid I'm developing multiple personality disorder. I'm the radio shrink's dream come true."

But there it was—a feeling of excitement, of freedom, even a barely remembered stirring of sensuality—and it had quite a grip on her. No matter how hard she tried to shake it off by reminding herself that she really *was* Gillian Hunter, Mother, Gillie Hanrahan, teenage girl, kept hanging on.

"Admit it," she told her reflection in the mirror when the blouse lay on the bed waiting for her as she took the hot rollers out of her hair. "It feels kind of good for a change. And it is only a lark, after all. Sunday night Lijah will be back and so will his mother."

She didn't remember when the last time was that she had left her hair loose. It was always braided or ponytailed or rolled into a bun to keep it neat, tidy and out of the way. But not tonight. Tonight she brushed it and let it fall in waves down her back.

As always she applied her makeup sparingly, her newfound daring side exerting itself only in a darker brown shade of eyeshadow and a second coat of mascara. She figured it was a trade-off since her cheeks had a natural color tonight that didn't need the enhancement of blush. A pale gloss left her lips merely shiny, and then she turned to that red blouse.

"You're stalling," she told herself when she put on her black slacks first.

A glance at the clock told her there was no more time for stalling. Kurt would be there to pick her up any minute.

Then she remembered perfume and went back to the dresser.

Actually, it wasn't perfume. Or even cologne. It was body fragrance, whatever that was. Robin had given it to her to wear to the How Singles Connect seminar. It was a light, clean scent that Gillie had not worn to the class. But for tonight. . . .

She dabbed just a little on her wrists, behind her ears and on her collarbones, and then started to put the top back on. She stopped. It was Gillie Hanrahan who unscrewed it again and put a drop just above where her bra dipped between her breasts.

Another glance at the clock. He was three minutes late. Even Gillie Hanrahan couldn't answer the door topless.

The red blouse was not silk but it felt the same. Cool and slinky, it slipped over her shoulders. There were no buttons or snaps to hold it closed, only the long trailing sash to wrap around her waist.

For a moment Gillie Hunter woke up. It was she who tied the sash so tightly she could hardly breath. The point of the V barely cleared the hollow of her throat.

"Well, that ruins it," Gillie Hanrahan told the reflection. The blouse looked like a red bandage supporting broken ribs and binding her small breasts into oblivion.

Watching the clock, she hurriedly retied the sash. This time the V was just deep enough to be alluringly seductive without actually showing anything.

Still, Gillian Hunter felt naked.

On the other hand, Gillie Hanrahan felt sexy.

When the doorbell rang at that instant, a thrill of excitement put Gillian Hunter back to sleep and the blouse stayed the way it was.

"Wow," Kurt said, wide-eyed and obviously impressed when Gillie let him in. "I'm not sure my talents as a chef warrant this."

Gillie just smiled as if she was accustomed to male admiration. "Come in while I get my coat." He reached it before she did. As he held it for her, she said, "You really didn't have to come and get me. I could have driven myself."

When the coat had slipped on over the silkiness of her blouse Kurt's hands settled onto her shoulders, his face dropping next to hers from behind. "And you smell wonderful," he said in a deep, raspy voice before he answered her. "The apartment complex is like a maze. I didn't want to take the chance of losing you in it. Call me antiquated, but I wouldn't have let you come home by yourself anyway. I would have followed you, so it only made sense for me to pick you up."

Charming and chivalrous, too. Gillie Hanrahan reveled in it.

They talked about Elijah on the short drive to the brown brick structures that made up Oakwood Apartments and the walk upstairs to the third floor of his building. But when Kurt had closed the door be-

hind them, the subject of the boy had been left outside, as if by silent agreement and Gillie and Kurt were
alone.

The apartment was especially warm after the frigid
winter air, and smelled of turkey. Kurt hit a switch
beside the door and light flooded the small kitchen
where serving dishes waited to be filled, covered pans
stood on each of the four stove burners, and a bottle
of wine chilled in a bucket of ice with two long-
stemmed glasses on either side. Gillie was struck by the
neatness of the kitchen and wondered if it was always
like this or if he had just cleaned for the occasion.

Kurt took her coat from her and hung it on a hook
of a hall tree. Then he led the way into the kitchen
through the dining room, where a drop-leaf table was
set for two.

"Not only did your mother teach you to bake bread,
but cook turkey, too?" Gillie marveled.

"The hour of truth," he mused as he poured wine
and handed her a glass. "As a matter of fact she didn't
teach me to *bake* bread, just to knead it. I was the
muscle, you see, and she was the brains. As for this
meal, I was hoping you wouldn't ask. But since you
did, ever notice that sign over the deli in the grocery
store: Complete Holiday Dinners? Well, they mean it.
I picked the whole thing up early this morning, along
with detailed instructions for how to reheat it all so it
tastes as if I really did cook it."

"I knew it," she said in a mock distaste. "You're a
fraud, Reynolds."

"Only in the kitchen."

"Need help?"

He slid a box of stick matches across the counter to her. "The best thing you can do for me is get out of my way, woman. And light the candles on the table."

There were six white tapers in a holder that looked like a spiral staircase. While Gillie lit them she glanced into the living room beyond. Though deep in shadow she could see a low-backed plaid couch, the coffee table Elijah was so thrilled to dine on, and a wall unit that held a large screen television and an elaborate stereo system. One of the shelves held picture frames and a snowy white teddy bear. When the candles were lit, she wandered that way.

"Are these of April?" Gillie asked unnecessarily, picking up a photograph of a little girl sitting on a rocking horse. She was the image of Kurt.

"The one and only," he said as he brought serving dishes to the table.

She set the picture down and picked up the teddy bear, rubbing her nose in its soft fur. She felt a stab of the sadness that must haunt him at not having more access to his daughter. "Is this for when she comes to visit?"

Kurt stopped on his way back to the kitchen. For a moment he didn't answer. When he did, his tone was solemn. "I bought two of them when she moved away—one for her to take and one for here so there would be something familiar when she came to stay with me. She's never seen that one." He paused, then, in a lighter tone of voice, changed the subject. "How's your work coming?"

Gillie got the message. She put the bear back on the shelf and went to stand at the end of the counter. "I'm doing all right. If I keep my nose to the grindstone I should finish up on Saturday.''

"Good. Depending on how late it is when you finish, we can celebrate with just dinner or dinner and a movie on Saturday night.''

"Is that right?'' she feigned indignation. At that moment she couldn't think of anything she would rather do to celebrate finishing her work than spending the evening with him.

"Yes, that's right,'' he mimicked as he passed with a platter of turkey, bending over to rub his nose in her hair much the way she had done with the teddy bear.

He was dressed in camel-colored slacks and a cream-colored shirt. He had rolled the sleeves up two cuffs, baring thick wrists sprinkled with wheat-colored hair. There was something about those wrists and those big hands that made her stomach do a flip.

She followed him to the table. "How can you be so sure that you won't be sick of me by the end of tonight and never want to see me again?'' Realizing suddenly that her glance had strayed to the firm rise of his derriere, she shook a mental finger at herself and went around him.

His smile was smug. "I'm not worried about you becoming one of the dates I could have lived without,'' he said theatrically. He turned off the kitchen light and held a chair for her. "Sit down before this meal I slaved over all day gets cold.''

"Dates you could have lived without?'' she repeated as she sat down.

"Mmm,'' Kurt mused, sitting across from her and holding out the platter of turkey to her. "The worst one I had was with a stockbroker. I picked her up and before we had even left her condominium she warned me that she judged men by their cars. 'You are what you drive,' she said. That put one strike against me because the Volvo was in the shop and I had borrowed a friend's Volkswagen Rabbit. She told me as she buckled her seat belt that said I was not very bold or aggressive and any intimate encounter with me would probably be short, fast and jerky, not the way she liked it at all. I found perverse pleasure in letting her believe I owned the car."

Gillie laughed and blushed at the same time, hoping her red cheeks were hidden by the dim light. "How did you meet this person?" Gillie managed as she laughed at him.

"A blind date, of course. How about you? You must have had some pretty good ones to put them on a par with a poke in the eye with a sharp stick?"

"Let's see. I've had seven dates in five years, not counting the two times Robin arranged for me to meet someone through a dinner or a party at her house. I could have lived without all of them."

"Present company excluded," he supplied.

"That goes without saying," she assured him. Strange how easy she was finding it to flirt. "Anyway, I'd say the worst was Robin's ophthalmologist. His ancestry had been traced back to an English lord whose family crest he wore on his blazer. From there he told me about his golfing expertise, illustrated by pulling down the neck of his sweater to show me the Professional Golfers' Association monogram on the shirt underneath and hiking up his pant leg for the

PGA monogram on his argyle socks. I started to get nervous about what his shorts might say and if he was going to drop his pants right there to show me.''

Kurt laughed, a sound she relished. Then he pushed his plate away, folded his forearms on the table and leaned toward her. "My shorts don't say anything."

She had opened herself up for that one. Gillie pushed her dish away, too. "My compliments to the chef, whoever he or she might have been."

His eyes held hers, sparkling with what looked like delight. When his smile came, it was filled with amusement at her obvious sidestep. But he let her off the hook. "What do you say we move this to the couch?"

With the raspy tone back in his voice, Gillie wasn't sure that was a safe change. She hedged, "Without doing the dishes?"

"They won't go anywhere." He pushed his chair away and stood up, reaching for her arm.

"You'll be sorry if you let these sit like this."

Kurt's arm came around her shoulders, he picked up the candle holder with his other hand, and guided her into the living room. "I'll chance it," he whispered into her ear.

They weren't her dishes, she told herself. And this wasn't her apartment or her holiday dinner. This was her lark. So why shouldn't she just enjoy getting up from the table and sitting on the couch—very closely—beside this man who made her feel new again?

He set the candles on the coffee table, their glow slightly illuminating the room. The yellow flames reflected in the glass of the sliding door that led to his balcony made it seem as if a dozen candles burned instead of just six.

His arm stayed around her as they sat on the couch, the heat of his hand through her sleeve, rubbing gently, radiated warmth all through her. "It really was a good meal," she said again for lack of anything else to say. Somehow her mind was suddenly too occupied with sensations to think of conversation. The couch was the soft sort that sank way down when they sat on it. Gillie seemed to fit perfectly into the curve of Kurt's body, as well, and together both feelings made it seem right that she was there.

"I was more interested in the company than the food," Kurt said.

Gillie could feel him watching her and she was drawn to meet his gaze. The candlelight gilded his handsome features. The sight turned the flame up on the feelings that were fast coming to life in her.

His raspy whisper came again, "I love the way you look, do you know that? With your hair loose I keep remembering that first morning we met in the parking lot. You've hardly been out of my thoughts ever since," he said.

"Giving you nightmares, am I?" she answered, meaning for it to be glib and instead hearing it come out a bit breathy.

"You're haunting me but it isn't in nightmares. Dreams and fantasies maybe, but not nightmares."

It gave her a little thrill to hear that. He had been in her thoughts and fantasies so much since they'd met it was gratifying to know she had had the same effect on him.

He tipped her chin up and his mouth slowly lowered to hers as lazily as if he had all the time in the world, as if he was savoring something very special.

Gillie had been reliving over and over again the kiss they had shared the past Saturday night, most often at night as she lay alone in the dark in her bed. But not once had it been as good as the real thing.

Kurt's arms closed around her and drew her up against his broad chest. His lips parted and his tongue entered her mouth, all warm and wet and tasting of wine. Gillie accepted it, met it. She filled her hands with the feel of him, of his wide back where muscles tensed beneath his shirt, of the hair at the nape of his neck.

Her body was alive and free and wanting in a way that had never been like this. When Kurt scooped her up and brought her to his lap she understood that he, too, was answering the need to be closer. The thick hardness that nudged her hip told her of desires that matched those burning ever hotter in her.

Their kisses grew urgent. Kurt's hand slipped beneath the shoulder of her blouse and slid both bra strap and silky fabric down her arm. The feeling of his hand on her bare skin was electric and wonderful, and she arched her back in a demand of her own.

His mouth left hers, trailing hungry kisses along her throat, across her collarbone and down the widening V of her blouse, stopping on the sensitive swell of her breast. Her head fell back and a small groan of passion escaped her as his hand smoothed the fabric away and took her flesh fully, kneading tenderly. He kissed his way back up to where her neck curved into her shoulder, and gently nibbled there.

Every inch of her body was alive and wanting, her nerves straining. Her nipples felt pinched, and as if he sensed her need, he squeezed them, then circled the sensitive areola. He rolled the nipple between his thumb and index finger, sending a sharp surge to the core of her.

Every bit as much as her body craved his touch, she craved touching him. She molded her palm on his neck and drew it lower, finding her way inside his shirt where coarse hair dusted his chest. The buttons popped open as she explored the solid expanse, reveling in the feel of his warm skin covering powerful muscles.

Still it was not enough. She wanted...needed...so much more. To feel the bare flesh of his back, of his hips and lower. To feel her own bare skin against his, to feel his weight...

Then, into the quiet broken only by the sound of their fast, shallow breathing, came the crash of metal against metal and breaking glass, followed by the screech of tires. And the cocoon passion was weaving around them was shattered.

Gillian Hunter woke up.

"No, stop," she managed from a throat constricted with desire.

Kurt drew back with a sound that was part sigh, part groan. "Damn whoever is out there," he said under his breath.

"It isn't that." Regret of her own sounded in the huskiness of her voice. "I just can't do this. Not to-night."

She heard him swallow, felt the warmth of another sigh in her hair. "Not tonight?"

"I'm afraid—" Now it was Gillie who needed to swallow. "I'm afraid it's not me who's choosing it."

"Gillie, I'm not forcing—"

"No, it isn't that. I'm just not myself."

His chuckle was kind but confused. "And I could have sworn this was you."

"I know it must sound crazy. I just don't want to regret this in the morning because I'm not thinking like myself tonight."

The sound he made was a bittersweet laugh. "I want you, Gillie. More than I've ever wanted anyone. But as much as I want you, I would never have you regret anything that happens between us."

"Things are so mixed up."

"Relax. I understand. Part of it, anyway. But be-lieve this, what's happening between us is right. I know it and I can wait until you do, too."

His compassion doubled her feelings for him and made it all the more difficult to continue to deny both herself and him. But as long as she couldn't be sure which part of her was choosing this, she had to.

"I think you'd better take me home."

For a moment he kept her on his lap, holding her. She sensed the force he was exerting over himself and her own willpower was sorely tested. Then the buzzer from the security door downstairs sounded.

He didn't respond to it instantly and for a moment Gillie wondered if he was going to answer it at all. Then he sighed heavily once more and finally let her go.

As she straightened her clothes, he crossed to the speaker, hit the button and barked, "What?"

"Mr. Reynolds? This is the manager. I'm afraid someone has rammed into your car and driven away."

Chapter Seven

By the next morning Gillie Hanrahan had disappeared. It was Gillian Hunter who sat at her drawing table all day and most of the evening on Friday, drawing satin shoes with velvet roses on the toes that matched the purse she had been working on the day before. The assignment was for an ad for holiday accessories that would run nationwide. But while her eyes and hands worked, her mind wandered to things other than expensive shoes.

Gillian Hunter was not so sure she actually would have regretted it if Gillie Hanrahan had gone through with what had begun on Kurt's couch the past night. In fact, the ending to their date had only made the man more attractive, more appealing, more desirable.

"How many people do you know would put the ramming of their expensive car second to the feelings of someone who had just caused them intense frustration?" she asked Rik where he sat beside her stool.

Kurt had paid only the briefest attention to the accident. The police were called but since the driver was long gone, there was virtually nothing that could be done. Through it all he had been more concerned with her, her feelings and his not having caused any damage to their relationship by moving too fast for her.

Amazing. Very flattering, and very nice.

Then he had driven her home, tenderly kissed her at the door, and left her with her own unquenched desires. Gillie Hanrahan may have gone to sleep unfulfilled, but it was Gillian Hunter who woke up, still unfulfilled and wanting him.

Biological need, she told herself over and over again.

But today she knew it was something more than that and she couldn't deny the feelings for him that were pushing a little harder against the lid she was sitting on to keep them under control. This man seemed perfect. A part of her couldn't help beginning to believe he actually was, in spite of the part of her that experience had taught to beware of what was underneath the way a person seemed.

When the white desk phone on her night table rang at ten that night Gillie was in her room, just about to go to bed. Without understanding how, she knew the call was from Kurt and alarms sounded in her head.

For a moment she didn't answer it; instead she stared as it rang once, twice....

Maybe she shouldn't answer it at all. Maybe she should hide rather than have anything to do with him, rather than running the risk....

Three times.

But the plain, unmitigated truth was that she didn't want to hide. She wanted to talk to him. She wanted to see him, to be with him, to have him make love to her. She didn't want to want any of that. But she did.

Four times.

Eventually the blush will come off the rose, she warned herself. And if her heart was involved when it did ...

Five times.

She wouldn't let her heart be involved, at least not as much as it had been twice before. And she wasn't going into this with her eyes closed the way she had both of those other times.

Gillie picked up the phone on the sixth ring. Kurt's deep, resonant voice rumbled through the line. "I didn't wake you, did I?"

"No, I was just—" Staring at the phone and wishing I didn't know you so I could be safe again, she finished silently. She cleared her throat. "I was just finishing up for the day."

"You're a dedicated woman."

"That's me all right."

"Did you really spend this whole day and night working?" he asked.

"No, I took Rik for a walk around the block at noon. Without Lijah to run him ragged he gets antsy. How about you?"

"No, I'm pretty used to not being run ragged by Elijah. I don't get antsy."

"I meant what did you do today?"

"I feel guilty telling you when you worked, but I sat on my duff and watched football games."

"Lazy, no good," she teased. It was terrible the way his voice tugged at her heart and lightened her spirits.

"Did you talk to our boy?"

"Twice. He's having a great time."

"And you're missing him so much you had to call him twice."

"It was a necessity. The first time I forgot to remind him to take his vitamin."

Kurt laughed and the sound made her smile. "That's a necessity all right."

Gillie got into bed, sitting propped against the plain oak headboard, and pulled the covers up to her breasts. The sheets felt especially smooth against her skin tonight and she was particularly sensitive to it. "How's your car?"

He groaned. "Looks a lot worse in the daylight. Luckily the dent is straight into the trunk so I can still drive it. It shouldn't take anything but body work to fix." He cleared his throat and finished in his own particular brand of sexiness. "Speaking of body work..."

Her toes curled and Gillie cut him off before he could go any further. "Did the manager turn up the culprit or a witness?"

Kurt chuckled but conceded to her swerve. "Apparently the car doesn't belong to any of the tenants."

"Maybe it was someone from your past. A jilted lover?" she suggested with mock suspicion.

"Well, it's hard to say," he played along. "I've left such a long string of them pining for me I just couldn't be sure which of the horde might have tracked me down." His tone became serious again. "Back to body work. I'd like to talk about what was going on before we were so rudely interrupted."

That made Gillie very uncomfortable. "I think having your car smashed is a little more than just rude," she hedged.

He ignored it. "So, who was I kissing on the couch last night?"

Gillie grimaced and didn't answer for a moment. "It was me," she finally admitted. "Then again, it wasn't."

"Of course. That clears it up perfectly," he said facetiously.

"It was me, only it was me about fifteen years ago."

"And that was bad, I take it."

"Not bad exactly. Just not who I am now."

"Who are you now?"

"I'm...Elijah's mother," she seized the only thing she could come up with.

"I think I'm getting the picture. And Elijah's mother isn't a woman. Is that why, twice now, when things heated up between us you bolted?"

"As I recall, the first time you agreed that it wasn't good to get carried away," she reminded him.

"Okay, you've got me on that score. It was a hold-over from the past two and a half years of being leery myself. I swore when someone asked me what my sign was I was going to say Proceed With Caution because that was exactly how I've felt since the end of my marriage. Until now."

For a moment he didn't say anything, as if waiting for her to think about that. Then he went on. "But everything about what's between us feels right. It's kismet. We're soulmates finding each other. Call it whatever you want, but I believe that that's what you and I are into here."

"I don't trust things like that," she said quietly.

"Things like what? Instincts?"

"Yes. Instincts are too limited, too...blind. They get confused and stifled by emotions, by needs, by necessity." And she was being too serious. She finished in a joking tone, "I think there should be personal résumés the way there are professional ones."

"Personal résumés?" he repeated, laughing.

"Sure. Apply for a job and you go in with your entire work history all spelled out and backed up with verifiable references and affidavits that phone calls can check out. If people in relationships had to submit one telling as much about their personal pasts, complete with names and numbers—"

"You show me yours and I'll show you mine," he offered lasciviously.

But Gillie was on a roll and she went on. "It's just that people are rarely what they seem to be and too often their true colors don't come out until after feelings and sometimes entire lives are involved."

"Okay," he agreed with more laughter in his voice. "What are you hiding?"

"Ah-ha, you see. If I had submitted a personal résumé you'd already know. We could both just refer to each other's references and—"

Kurt's voice turned somewhat more serious. "This is really something you've thought about, isn't it? Why is that?"

"I told you, it just seems practical."

He was back to being theatrical. "Do you think I have some deep, dark secrets that are going to lunge out at you when you least expect it?"

That was exactly what she thought because that was exactly what she had experienced, but she couldn't admit it. "I'm just saying," she went back to what had gotten them into this in the first place, "that I don't believe instincts give us some mystical power. I think they're based on what we see and that we don't always see what's really there."

"I don't know if I understand that, or agree with it. But I do know that I trust what I see and I trust my instincts."

"But what you thought was me last night wasn't, and you didn't have any way of knowing that, of knowing what was going on inside of my head," she said to prove her point.

"You're wrong."

"You read minds and you never told me?" she joked.

But Kurt's answering tone was not teasing. "I didn't know what was going on in your head last night, no. What I do know is that it's been so long since you've let yourself be a woman that when that part surfaces it scares the hell out of you and it seems like it must not really be you at all. But I don't buy that. In my opinion, rather than suppressing it, that part needs some special nurturing to bring it back to where it's supposed to be so you can be a mother *and* a woman.''

''Have you been listening to the shrink show?''

He laughed but didn't let her off the hook. ''Tell me how long it's been since you let a man make love to you?'' he added with so much compassion, so much tenderness, that she couldn't take offense. Then before she could answer he said, ''Let me guess. At least five years. Is there anything you do just for yourself, Gillie? I don't think so. Instead you wear yourself out with devoted single parenting and working to make ends meet. Don't get me wrong, I admire that. More, I respect it. But there has to be a little left over somewhere for you or you're going to die inside. I know what your true colors are. They're there to see for anyone who cares enough to look. And I care. A lot. Be a mother for Elijah. But just be yourself for me . . . and for you.''

Gillie didn't know what to say to that so instead she said, ''Does this mean you don't need to see my personal résumé?''

This time he did joke back, gently, ''How many pages is it?''

''Only four.''

''I can hardly wait,'' he answered facetiously. ''Guess I'll have to start compiling mine so you can relax. First you think I'm some sort of child abuser-kidnapper and now you think I'm Jack the Ripper disguised as a regular guy. But be warned that in order to defend myself I'm going to include every tribute, testimonial, plaudit, commendation and kudo I've received."

"Just don't leave out the criticisms and complaints."

"And the phone numbers so they can all be verified," he reminded. "But in the meantime, while I'm getting this all together, do you have any idea when you'll finish up tomorrow so I can plan our evening?"

The rush of eager anticipation that suggestion sent through her couldn't be ignored. "I'll be done sometime in the afternoon," she told him.

"Great. Then we can take in a movie, too. Can you be ready by six?"

"I think so. If not I'll make you clean my brushes while you wait."

"It's a deal." He cleared his throat and teased, "Oh, and Gillie? It's a come-as-you-are date."

She understood the double meaning in that. With the wild sensations he always brought to life in her it was a taller order than he realized. But again she teased, "Remember that you asked for it. Blue jeans and a turtleneck are the real me."

"Perfect. I'm going to hold you to it," he rasped out in that husky, sensual tone again. "Good night, love."

"Good night," she barely managed with what was left of her breath after he had taken it away with the timbre of his voice and the endearment.

As she put the receiver back in the cradle she wondered at how easily he could turn her into a hundred and five pound hormone. Then she turned the light off, rolled onto her stomach and tried not to think about how empty her bed seemed.

It was after five the next day when Gillie took a step back from her drawing table to judge the completed layout. She decided she had pulled it off.

She set her brushes to soak and was headed back to her room to get ready when the doorbell rang.

"You're early, Reynolds," she said as she unlocked the screen door and let Kurt in.

"I know. I couldn't wait another minute to see you." He kissed her lightly on her ear and closed the door after himself.

He was dressed in a cream-colored turtleneck sweater and tight jeans. He turned around to drop his leather bomber jacket on the couch, and Gillie's gaze got stuck on the back pockets that rode his derriere. They were still at that level when he turned abruptly and she hastily jerked her glance from his zipper.

"Giving me the once over, Hunter?" he asked in a tone that said he certainly hoped so.

Caught in the act Gillie surprised herself by managing to play it cool. "I was just thinking that I could use you as a model for my next assignment. It's a jeans ad."

"And I thought it was personal interest," he said letting her know he still believed it was. Then he spread his arms. "At your service. I love to be used."

"Careful I might take you up on it. It would save me having to hire a model."

"I'm game."

The question was, how could she keep her mind on her work? "Make yourself at home while I get ready," she said, rather than taking their discussion further.

"You look great the way you are." His gaze went slowly down her black turtleneck to her jeans and then back up. He feigned a menacing expression and said, "I like you in black and blue." Then he gasped melodramatically. "Oh, no, I'm showing my evil true colors. Cancel that."

"You're a laugh riot a minute. Did you come to take me out or to make fun of the innovative ideas that make me ahead of my time?"

"Both. Get those great buns of yours in gear so we can go eat. I'm starved."

"Now the truth comes out. It wasn't that you couldn't wait another minute to see me at all."

"Found out." He turned her by the shoulders toward the hall that led to the bedrooms and gave her a swat on the rump. "Go."

She saluted and headed down the hall. "Make yourself comfortable."

As she freshened her blush and put on mascara, Gillie wondered at her relaxed mood. There was always this feeling of elation, of accomplishment, of freedom when she had finished a project, especially when it had been a particularly demanding one. But today there was also a sense of what Kurt had spoken about on the phone the past night—of their being right together.

She knew that should worry her. And it did. She knew she should be looking for clues to what the surface hid. And she was. But for tonight she decided to give herself a break. After all, this was the end of a holiday weekend as well as a grueling work schedule, she had earned a relaxed evening.

On impulse she brushed her hair out, letting it fall in the full waves caused by being tightly braided all day. With fresh lip gloss as the final touch to her laid-back appearance, Gillie left her bedroom and found Kurt studying the wall that separated the living room from the kitchen. She had decorated it with a pale flowered wallpaper halfway up, a chair rail, a grape vine wreath, a dozen of so family pictures and several shelves, some holding knickknacks and others bracing books she was always meaning to read and never seemed to get around to.

As she came down the hall he spoke to her but kept his eyes on the family photos. "I like your house, have I told you that before?"

"No, but thanks."

"It's a warm place. Homey. Meant to be lived in."

"With a ten-year-old boy and a dog around, there isn't much choice," she deflected the compliments.

"Sure there is. April lives in her mother's pristine palace where there's never a piece out of place or an unprofessional photograph in sight, let alone a blurred picture of a dog—" he leaned closer "—and someone's thumb. I'll bet Elijah took that one."

"He's very proud of it," Gillie conceded with a laugh.

"So you framed it and hung it in a prominent place in the living room. You're a good lady, do you know that?"

"I know I'm a hungry one. What's up for tonight?"

"Where do you stand on Chinese food?"

"I'm a fiend for egg rolls."

"Good, I'm dying for it. And then I thought we'd take in the movie at the Esquire. It's foreign, mostly in black and white and has subtitles, and I understand it's really good," he said as he held her coat for her.

They ate at a place called the China Doll, a dimly lit hole-in-the-wall. Though Gillie had never been there before it was obviously an Arland hot spot because it seemed as though everyone in the place was a parent of a high school student. The drawback of a small community was that every one of them felt inclined to say hello to the principal.

"I feel like I'm out with a celebrity," Gillie managed between interruptions and introductions that left any continuous conversation impossible.

When they were finished with dinner they drove to the Esquire. It was a classic old theater, complete with a balcony, which was where Kurt and Gillie sat.

As a rule, Gillie didn't like reading her movies. But in spite of the subtitles, she came away loving the film. Kurt didn't think as highly of it, which inspired a lively, good-natured discussion on the way home. Then, before she had thought twice about it, they were back at her house and she had invited him in for a glass of wine.

"So, who are you tonight, lady?" he teased as he came up from behind her in the kitchen and circled her shoulders with his arms.

"Ginger Rogers?" she joked back, pouring the rosy liquid into two goblets on the counter in front of her.

"No, don't be her, I'm too lousy a dancer to be Fred Astaire. How about just Gillie Hunter, femme fatale?" The tip of his nose traced a path through her hair.

"Femme fatale? Me? Right," she said facetiously, her own voice husky with the feelings that were coming to life within her.

"A femme fatale is an irresistibly attractive woman. I have been finding you irresistibly attractive all night long." He nuzzled her ear, his breath a hot gust.

Gillie wondered how she was going to drink the wine through the constriction in her throat. He was rapidly turning her whole body into a tautly strung cord, as only he could do. With great effort she managed to tease back. "Sure, Thanksgiving I dress to the nines and you barely pay me any attention at all. Tonight it's jeans and a sweater and I'm irresistible. Go figure."

He kissed the sensitive spot just below her ear and behind her jaw, sending a shiver through her. "Barely paid you any attention at all? If that's what you considered Thanksgiving I'm going to have to go to great lengths to pay you some attention."

His voice was a deep, raspy timbre. Gillie felt his tongue flick her earlobe and little shards of glittering gold scattered inside her. He moved the circle of his arms farther down, kissing his way inside her turtleneck. His arms pressed her breasts in a hint of things to come, making her nipples hard. His hands rubbed her upper arms in a slow, soothing motion. The breath came into her lungs thickly and between her legs there started an ache of emptiness.

Then Kurt stepped to her side, scooped up both glasses of wine and went into the living room.

For a moment Gillie just stood there, a bit dumbstruck, a lot wanting. She took a deep pull of air as if it would wake her from a trance, and followed him. He was at one end of the couch, his glass in his hand, her wine waited for her in the dead center of the coffee table.

Confused, Gillie picked it up and sat on the middle cushion of the sofa, slightly more toward him than away from him. She hooked the toes of her plain, flat shoes on the edge of the coffee table. "Would you like a fire?" she asked, her confusion obvious in her tone.

Kurt stared at her for a moment before answering, his green eyes piercing, his mouth in a Cheshire cat smile. "You mean in the fireplace?" he said finally. "No, I don't think so."

Gillie noticed that he had kicked off his brown loafers. He stretched his long legs out, resting his heel very near to her feet. Still watching her, he took a sip of wine.

Gillie felt expectation in the air, she just didn't know what he expected. All she did know was that her body did not want to be sitting a cushion away from his.

"Where's the dog?" he asked in a way that sounded ridiculously suggestive and intimate.

"Asleep on Lijah's bed, I'm sure. He won't move a muscle until morning."

"Good."

Gillie swallowed. It was as if he was stroking her with his eyes, with his voice. But not with anything else. She felt very frustrated and she didn't have the slightest idea what to do or say.

After what seemed like an eternity of his staring at her, he finally broke the silence. "I guessed, but you didn't tell me if I was right."

"About what?"

"About it being five years since a man has made love to you."

Again she swallowed, with some difficulty. "Eight," she heard herself admit, and then wished she hadn't.

"Eight?" he repeated in surprise.

"How long has it been for you?" she shot back before he could ask more.

"It hasn't been eight years," he answered gently and somewhat incredulously before saying, "A couple of months."

Gillie's heart was beating so hard she could feel it. Somehow she hadn't given his sex life a thought. Now something struck her. "Was she someone you—" She couldn't finish. If she said "cared for" and his answer was no it would make him someone who slept with women he had no feelings for. If his answer was yes then maybe he wasn't over those feelings. Why hadn't she asked about relationships other than marriages before?

"Was she someone I what?" he prompted.

Gillie shrugged and doubted—him, herself, what her body was crying out for.

"Was she someone I loved?" he guessed.

Gillie answered with only a raise of her eyebrows.

"She was someone I respected. Someone I liked. But not someone I cared about the way I do you."

"And now?" Gillie managed tensely.

"Now she's involved with someone else and so am I. And I'm happy for us both."

Gillie lifted her head in a slight nod and silence fell again. She felt very warm. "Why are you sitting so far away?" The words slipped out in a sensuous sounding voice she barely recognized as her own.

"I'm not," he told her matter of factly. "You are."

He trailed one toe from her instep up to her ankle, inside her pant leg. It was torture when she wanted so much more.

"I've done all the pressing," he said, kindly but firmly. "I won't do any more. You know I want you."

The unspoken end to that was that he didn't know if she wanted him. And how could he when twice now she had panicked and bolted. But even with the ball in her court Gillie wasn't sure she knew how to play the game. What she did know was that if he didn't hold her, kiss her, touch her very soon, she would die.

"It's just me here tonight," she said by way of beginning, her legs accommodating his foot as it wandered up her calf on the outside of her jeans.

"Good," he repeated. "I wouldn't want anyone else. And I wouldn't want you to be uncertain and have regrets."

It surprised her to realize that there was no uncertainty tonight. None at all. She leaned forward and put her wineglass on the table but once it was there she didn't know what to do with herself. Rather than sitting back, she hugged her bent knees, sighed and looked over at Kurt, hoping he would get the message.

One of his eyebrows rose in question. "Say it."

For a moment she couldn't speak. She couldn't breathe. But there was so much need running through her body that in the end she would have walked through hot coals to have him. "I want you, Kurt," she whispered, looking him straight in those magnificent green eyes of his.

His handsome face blossomed into a smile as sexy as any she had ever seen. He sat forward and set his glass on the table. Then he reached his hand out for her to take.

Gillie didn't hesitate. She slipped her hand in his and when he squeezed she squeezed back. He stood up and pulled her with him. As they passed the front door he reached, turned the lock, then flicked off the light.

The darkness lent Gillie courage and she led the way to her bedroom. One part of her wondered what in the world she was doing, while another part wondered why she had waited so long.

Pale winter moonlight faintly illuminated the room. Kurt closed the door and, for Gillie, the rest of the world was closed out, too. He came up behind her and folded his arms around her. He caught the points of her breasts in his embrace, the taut nipples responding with a straight shot of desire like a lightning bolt to the center of her. Rather than merely hugging her, he pressed her tightly against him, his own desire for her a hard ridge at the base of her spine.

Gillie took a bumpy breath and reached her hands up to his arms where they pressed the sides of her breasts. She let her head rest back on his chest, reveling in the clean woodsy scent that was all his own. She had never wanted anyone as much as she wanted him.

He kissed her ear, her jaw, and she arched her neck to accommodate him. She caressed his arms, kneading him in the way her body was yearning to be until he loosened his grip and both of his hands slipped to her breasts in answer.

The sharp intake of her breath became a groan of pleasure and on their own her hands covered his and pressed them more firmly against her flesh, arching her back at the same time.

He turned her to face him, his mouth finding hers, open and searching. His tongue darted in and pulled out, and Gillie matched him thrust for thrust. She filled her hands with his broad back, the muscles rolling under her palms, and then she slid lower, squeezing the tight mounds of that derriere that so often caught her eye. Kurt's hands traveled a similar path, and when he had cupped her rear he pulled her hips up and dipped his own so that the now familiar ridge left her with no doubt about his needs or his intentions.

He let go of her and found his way to the front of her jeans. He popped the button and opened the zipper. His hands sliding inside to hold her hips.

Gillie had a flash of self-consciousness as she felt her jeans drop just below her waist. It had been eight years since a man had seen her.

He must have felt her tense because he pulled his hands out and merely let his thumbs ride the waistband. Even his kiss became less urgent, less hungry, slower. But self-conscious or not, that wasn't the pace she needed and with a tiny sound deep in her throat she found the hem of his sweater and pushed her way up underneath it, all the way to his shoulders.

An understanding chuckle sounded from him as he broke away from their kiss and let her take the sweater off.

"You realize, of course, that one good turn deserves another," he whispered lasciviously in her ear as he divested her of her turtleneck and bra.

Then his mouth was on hers again before dropping to her chin, to the arch of her throat, to the hollow. His tongue traced the sharpness of her collarbone. By the time the warm wetness reached her breast she felt weightless and she welcomed his sliding her jeans and silky panties off.

He was right—turnabout was fair play. And regardless of how wonderful he looked in his jeans, there was no way she was going to leave him in them. Sight was not the sense she needed satisfied at that moment.

Gillie found his snap and zipper, struggled a little with them and then, giving in to a need she had been suppressing for a long while, she pushed her hands down the back of his unfastened jeans and learned the texture of his backside. Down slipped the last barrier that separated them. At last the softness of her body pressed fully against the long, hard length of his, and her every nerve was alive at once.

In the small room the bed was only a step away and she wasn't even aware of taking it before they were lying there, their tongues once again parrying, his hands working their magic on her breasts and his leg wrapped tightly around hers so that the softness of her stomach yielded to the rigid swell of him.

Stronger than her need to be touched was her desire to feel him inside her. She arched her hips against his, her mouth escaping him.

"Now, Kurt, now," she barely breathed out.

It only took half a roll for his weight to be fully on her, his body to find the perfect position between her thighs, opened in answer to the need that drove them both to a near frenzy. And then he was there, at the very opening of her, probing, teasing, entering.

Once he was inside her, Gillie wrapped her legs around him and met him thrust for thrust, until something within her exploded—so fiercely she wasn't sure she would survive it, so wonderfully she didn't care if she didn't. And just as the explosion was calming to smaller bursts she felt him stiffen and plunge deeply once, twice, three times, until he, too, was spent.

For a precious moment they laid still, melded together, as if they were meant to be one. Then, little by little, muscles relaxed, tautness eased, and breathing came again.

Kurt kissed her forehead. "How are you?" he whispered.

"Wonderful," she answered, unable to keep astonishment out of her voice.

He left her then, bringing her close to his side in one smooth motion. His other arm came around her, holding her, stroking her back.

A heavy fatigue settled through her, her arms and legs felt weighted, and her body seemed to melt into his. All Gillie could think of was that the date he could have lived without had been very, very wrong—there was nothing short, fast or jerky about his lovemaking, and certainly nothing lacking in boldness.

And then, having found something she had long been missing, she fell asleep.

Chapter Eight

Gillie had regrets in the morning all right. Except that 1:00 a.m. was just barely morning and her regrets were not for what had happened between them, but for the fact that Kurt was asleep when she wanted it to happen again.

She didn't know what exactly had awakened her. Maybe it was the strangeness of having someone in her bed or her instinctive response to the feel of him holding her even as he slept, his body big and warm and hard. Or maybe it was the dream she'd been having about their lovemaking. But whatever the cause, she was wide awake and wanting him more than she had before.

She took a breath and breathed out. Maybe she could ignore the needs that were asserting themselves and go back to sleep.

Go away... go away....

But there was a taut yearning all through her body that stubbornly stayed on.

How had she made it go away for the past eight years? she asked herself.

But she knew the answer. It hadn't been as difficult because there hadn't been as much to make go away.

With the two men she had been intimate with, making love had been nice. That was all, just nice. Until tonight she had never known just how wonderful it could be. And she wanted to feel it again.

Her nipples were so sensitive she couldn't bear to have them rubbing against Kurt's side. The aching emptiness between her legs certainly wasn't going away and wasn't likely to as long as she was this close to his naked body. As far as she could tell, she had two choices. Either wake him up and explain that she would really like to have a second helping of this delicacy she had just discovered tonight, or move as far away from him as she could and hope some higher power would have mercy and let her go back to sleep.

Waking him up seemed too... too forward, too immodest, too pushy, too—all right, it was sexist and archaic—unfeminine. So Gillie opted for moving away. She had barely broken the seam of their contact when Kurt's arms tightened around her and pulled her back.

He sighed. "What time is it?" he asked groggily.

"A little after one," she said without even trying to hide the fact that she was wide awake.

"You were asleep before I was. How come you're not now?"

"I just woke up," was all she would admit to.

"Mmm."

She laid very still, not knowing what to do. Then his voice came again in the darkness, sounding more alert. "The trouble with eating Chinese food and then…burning it off, is that when you wake up in the middle of the night you're starving."

Gillie agreed about starving but Chinese food had nothing to do with it. Still she could hardly tell him what she was hungry for. "I have some hot dogs in the refrigerator," she offered instead.

He groaned. "The only way I like them is cooked outdoors, charred black on the outside. Maybe if we just lie here we can go back to sleep."

That was the worst idea she had ever heard. "I have a gas barbecue that I cook on all winter. If you're game I am."

He laughed. "You're nuts. Get out of this warm bed at one in the morning and stand outside in zero degree temperatures to cook hot dogs?"

"We could roast marshmallows, too," she tempted.

He sighed and she thought he was going back to sleep. But just when she had about given up hope he sighed again. "I must be crazy. Let's do it."

Moments later, dressed only in his jeans and bomber jacket, Kurt was a delectable sight that occupied Gillie's attention. His was on the hot dogs and shifting from one bare foot to the other on the cold cement of her back patio.

"Feed me that marshmallow before you drop it. Are you falling back to sleep on me or what?" he asked.

"Guess my mind is wandering," she said, then blew on the marshmallow to cool it. She wore only her terry-cloth bathrobe, zipped to her neck. Her own feet were bare, as well, but she didn't notice the cold. "Open up," she instructed as she aimed for his mouth, wishing to follow the path there with her own. She watched jealously as his lips closed around the golden brown puff.

"There goes another one," he observed wryly as the marshmallow on the toasting fork fell down into the coals.

Gillie dragged her eyes off his Adam's apple. His beard was just beginning to show, his hair was sleep tousled and he looked rugged and heart-stoppingly sexy. "Oh well, having dessert first is bad for you anyway. Aren't those things about done?" She nodded at the hot dogs.

"Not yet. I told you I like them charred."

Gillie put two more marshmallows on the forks and watched him switch feet again.

"So," he said then in a perfectly conversational, matter-of-fact tone, "did you know that I'm falling in love with you?"

At first she didn't think she had heard him right. Then she decided he must be joking. "I'll bet you say that to all the girls you cook hot dogs with in the middle of the night."

"Since you're the only girl I've ever cooked hot dogs with in the middle of the night you're right."

There was still no gravity to his tone but Gillie was fast losing hope that he wasn't serious. She suddenly paid close attention to her marshmallows. "This one is perfect. Want it?"

Kurt shook his head. "I had the last one. You take it."

She did, glad that eating made speaking impossible. Her heart was racing, and her brain had stopped functioning.

Kurt turned the hot dogs. "So," he repeated in the same way, "am I shaping up better than a poke in the eye with a sharp stick in your book?"

Gillie swallowed the marshmallow and admitted quietly, "Yes. A lot better." Right away she fed him the other marshmallow and just as he swallowed it she said again, "Aren't those things done yet?"

Kurt picked one up and studied it, seeming not to think anymore about their conversation. "Good enough I guess. My feet are too cold to stand out here anymore. Whose idea was this, anyway?"

"Yours," she accused over her shoulder as she grabbed up the bag of marshmallows and held the door for him.

They took their food to the bedroom and by silent agreement left the light off, shed clothes and slipped back into the bed, sitting side by side. Gillie couldn't think of anything but what he'd said and he didn't even seem to remember it. Maybe it had been a joke after all.

"You're not eating," he observed after he'd polished off his second hot dog. He nodded at the almost whole one Gillie held in one hand while the other gripped the sheet and blankets to cover her bare breasts. It occurred to her that it was a measure of how far he had thrown her off balance that she didn't feel embarrassed to have climbed naked into bed with him to eat hot dogs.

"Oh. I guess I've had enough. Want to finish it?"

"Uh-huh, in a minute." He pulled her between his legs. His touch and the feel of his bare skin against her back did crazy things to her body.

He guided her hand over her shoulder to take a bite of the hot dog she still held. When he had swallowed it he spoke into her hair. "I've been wondering how I was going to tell you about my feelings," he went on as if there had been no break in the conversation that had begun outside. "If I had said it before we made love you might have figured it was a line to get you into bed. If I said it once we were here you might have thought it was in the heat of passion. I didn't want anything to detract from it." He paused and helped her feed him another bite of hot dog. "I also know it takes you by surprise so I don't expect you to say anything. I just wanted you to know where I stand."

He took the remaining hot dog out of her hand and set it on the night table. Then he slid down slightly so that she was resting very firmly against him.

"Now," he said as he began to nibble her neck and shoulders. "Back to what you woke me up for in the first place."

That made her laugh and broke some of the tension that had been building in her. "I beg your pardon. I did not wake you up."

"Of course you did. One minute I was sound asleep with a warm woman wrapped around me and the next I was abandoned and woke up in a room filled with sexual tension."

"A room filled with sexual tension?" she repeated dubiously and then played innocent. "What made you think that?"

"Part of those instincts I trust and you don't." He pressed his hips to her backside and smoothed his hands down her thighs, his arms rubbing seductively across her already taut nipples. "You did wake up hungry for more than a late-night barbecue, didn't you?"

"Mmm," was the only spoken admission he was going to get. Her body had instantly come alive. She ran her hands down the hard roughness of his thighs.

"You know," he mused as his palms slid up the sides of her stomach and each cupped a breast, "for someone who practiced celibacy for eight years I'd have thought once would have been enough for tonight, sort of an easy breaking in."

She supposed it was a response to his talk of his own feelings, but those that were washing through Gillie at that moment were not all sensual. Along with the undeniable fact that her body craved him physically was the knowledge that she cared about this man. Maybe more than cared. But she couldn't tell him that. She was afraid to admit it even to herself. His earlier declaration certainly couldn't be answered with one of her own and so she gave him something else. "I don't know if it matters to you..."

The softness of her voice must have told him what she was saying wasn't easy for her and didn't need to be made anymore complicated, for his hands slipped up to her shoulders and he just held her tenderly as she went on.

"But making love was never like this for me before. It was okay, nice, but not...like this."

His arms around her tightened and again he lowered his mouth to the curve of her shoulder, his breath warm there. When he spoke, his voice was a whisper. "And you think that might not matter to me? Gillie—" He laughed gently before adding, "It matters," in a tone that told her just how much.

For a long moment he just held her. Then he turned her to face him, slid them both down under the covers and found her mouth with his.

Eager to feel again what she had missed for so long and emboldened by the fact that she had finally found it, she explored his body. With both of her hands she sought his nipples, reveling in their hardening response. She slid her palms down his flat belly to that other hardness, straining for her as much as she was straining for him.

Their tongues parried, then their mouths parted to play other games at ears, at shoulders, at nipples and at navels. His hands found her, his fingers tantalized her while his tongue and teeth worked their way down in the same direction.

He surprised them both by finding a spot on her side, at the deepest dip of her waist, that was extraordinarily sensitive, and she learned that he liked to be stroked on the insides of his thighs.

Passion mounted and with it urgency. Gillie didn't think she could bear to wait another moment to feel him inside her, to climb to that glorious peak again.

Not a moment after she thought it, he spread her legs and came into her in one steady, even thrust as if fitting a missing piece into a puzzle. Together they moved, first slowly, then faster, building, growing in a crescendo of perfect harmony until for the second time that night fireworks and lightning bolts exploded inside Gillie, again and again, until she was spent and weak with the wonder of it.

Still joined but both exhausted, he rolled until she was on top of him. He covered them with the sheet and blankets that had worked down the bed, sighed and said again, "It matters, love. It matters."

Sunday got off to a late start. Without there seeming to be any question that they would spend the day together, the first thing they did was roll Gillie's drawing into a mailing tube for express-mailing tomorrow. With that accomplished they had breakfast at The Delectable Egg, a small restaurant in one of the renovated buildings on Market Street.

Seated next to an artwork-lined rustic brick wall they shared bacon, eggs, potatoes and toast, and tried to guess what the abstract watercolor beside their table was supposed to depict. Kurt thought it was the inside of a drainage pipe and Gillie argued that the earth tones made it a view into a cave.

Every so often, Kurt's hand strayed under the table to her thigh for a momentary squeeze or he draped his arm across the back of her chair and leaned very near for a bite off her fork instead of his. His actions seemed as natural as breathing and Gillie forgot about being careful or sitting on the lid of her feelings for this man.

It was after noon by the time they left The Delectable Egg and headed for a warehouse sale. Gillie would never have gone on her own, but with Kurt driving it became an adventure to find the concrete structure where the advertised spectacular sale on televisions, stereos, video games and equipment was taking place.

The whole reason for taking the assignment that had kept her busy over the Thanksgiving holiday was to earn extra money to buy Elijah a video game system for Christmas. Gillie and Kurt spent nearly two hours fighting the crowd in the warehouse and trying to find someone who could explain what exactly came with the set and what needed to be bought extra. By her third apology for dragging him into this mess Kurt ground out in her ear that he didn't mind, just before he took a nibble out of her lobe. At that moment they finally got a salesperson to pay some attention but Kurt's arm stayed around her shoulders and before she knew it, Gillie's was around his waist.

With the dented trunk of Kurt's Volvo filled with Elijah's Christmas present they headed for the airport. Sitting in the waiting area, Kurt laced his fingers through hers, covered her hand with his other hand and kept it nested against his stomach. The flight was delayed and to pass the time, he invented outrageous histories for the people around them.

Elijah and another boy who looked to be about a year younger were the first passengers off the plane when it landed. Escorted by a stewardess, Gillie's son bid the woman goodbye as if they were old friends and was quick to brag that he and the other boy had gotten to sit in the first-class section all the way home. Wriggling out of his mother's hugs, he accepted Kurt's hand on his shoulder with an affectionate shrug, not seeming in the least surprised to see Kurt with Gillie. He launched into a minute-by-minute account of his trip as they collected his bags and headed to White Fence Farm for a homecoming dinner of Elijah's favorite fried chicken.

Once home, the boy pleaded for Kurt to stay until he unpacked his suitcase and found the San Diego Zoo pennant he'd bought him. Elijah needn't have bothered because Gillie and Kurt had already arranged that Kurt would come in and wait until the boy was asleep so they could sneak his Christmas present into the basement.

Then, before she knew where the time had gone, it was after ten, Elijah was asleep, the video game was safely locked in a room downstairs and there was no more reason for Kurt to linger.

Never in her life had Gillie wanted someone to stay as much as she wanted him to at that moment.

"This has been the best twenty-four hours I've spent in recent memory," he said to her as he picked up his coat. "It felt good, just the two of us and then with Elijah, as if we were a family."

She had felt it, too. Enjoyed it all, too. Too much, she thought now that it was hurting her to have him leave. That ache was a reminder to her. "I don't know too many people who would call that mess we were in at the warehouse this afternoon a good time," she answered, trying to keep things light.

"I'd like to have more of it," he said sincerely, ignoring both her comment and her over-cheerfulness.

"More crowded warehouses? Now that is weird," she purposely misunderstood.

Kurt pulled her close. His hand rode her hip and he looked down into her face with those eyes that always seemed to see through her. "I think I know what you're doing here, Gil. You're distancing yourself, I imagine because you think it's safer. I looked at my divorce like a broken leg I needed to recover from. It taught me to be more careful, not to give up walking. I'm not sure you learned the same lesson."

She glanced down to the floor and then back up at him. "I'm still on my feet." But regardless of how carefree she wanted to appear, inside she was crying out for this day not to end. She put her hand on his hip, filled with the need to touch him, to complete the circuit and connect with him the way he was staying connected with her. But again her words and impersonal tone covered what she was feeling. "Thanks for taking me to the sale and picking Lijah up and... everything."

He didn't respond right away. Instead he searched her face as if reading something there. She knew that he saw her reticence to take the closeness between them any further, and had the impression that because of it he didn't say what he had intended to. He also didn't answer her thanks. "You're on your feet all right, but I'm not sure you're walking. I'd like it if you'd take those first few steps and give it a shot."

"Well, get your résumé in and I'll take it under consideration," she answered glibly, hoping it hid the clash going on inside her between panic and... And what? Love? The panic gained ground at that thought.

"Consider it, Gillie. My instincts are telling me this is absolutely right. If you can't trust your own, then trust mine." He kissed her then, softly, sweetly, forestalling any more of her glibness.

She wanted to melt into him, to take his hand and pull him with her to the bedroom, to never let him go. She fought it all.

When the kiss ended, Kurt shrugged into his jacket and opened the door. "I'll call you tomorrow," he said as he left.

Gillie locked up, turned out the lights and then sat in the recliner in the dark.

What exactly did she feel for this man?

A lot. More than she wanted to feel. Much, much more.

If only he was actually as terrific as he seemed she could welcome it. But how did a person ever really know what was going on inside another person's head? What truth might be lying beneath the surface? Phil had seemed terrific until after they were married. And she would have sworn that Paul was a wonderful guy who would have stuck by her side through anything. But then his real character had come out and nearly destroyed her.

"Maybe I should take a course in aura reading," she whispered, wishing she knew a way to see a person's true colors. "There must be some technique."

She thought about Kurt, about what she knew of him, wondering if there was a chink in his armor, a clue as to what, if anything, might be a hidden part of his character.

Nothing came to mind. He was wonderful. He was perfect. It was tempting to just relax and let her feelings for him run free the way they wanted to.

But her past experiences had been far too harsh for her to let her guard down completely yet.

A few dates, a few conversations, and twenty-four hours of bliss weren't any guarantee that it was safe for her to give in to her emotions.

Kurt might be right, she thought as she headed for bed. She was standing on her feet again but she wasn't altogether sure about taking those steps that led back into love. Maybe she was playing it too safe, but Gillie decided to plop back down hard on the lid of her feelings for him rather than chance too much too soon.

Chapter Nine

Kurt called Gillie on Monday night but he kept the conversation light. He could sense her skittishness and he didn't want to frighten her by pushing things too fast.

On Tuesday he and Elijah had their bachelor's dinner and Kurt began to realize that he cared as much about Gillie's son as he did about Gillie. Their big brother relationship had resulted in a rapport between them and Kurt couldn't help feeling as if he had found, in a convoluted manner, the family he was meant to have.

It was a strain not saying anything to Gillie when he brought Elijah home and shared a nightcap with her. He wanted to tell her he loved her, that he loved her son, but he still sensed her reticence and so he refrained and engaged in superficial conversation.

Slow and steady, he decided on the way home. As strong as his instincts were that what was happening between them was meant to be, he also knew instinctively that she was feeling the same things about him that he was feeling about her, regardless of whether or not she admitted it. She wasn't rejecting him. Whenever he kissed her, she kissed him back. Whenever he touched her, she accepted it, moved into it, touched him back. But obviously her scars from the past were deep and it was taking her a little more time to openly accept love back into her life. He didn't like it, but he could wait. She was worth it.

Gillie had invited him for dinner on Thursday night before he went for the weekend in Connecticut, and on that day, Kurt was humming when he came home after work to change clothes. A quick shower, a second shave, and he'd be on his way.

When the phone rang he was inside his closet hanging up his tie. He reached for the receiver and said, "Hello," as he sat on the edge of the bed and pulled off his right shoe.

"Is this Kurt Reynolds?" asked a woman's voice he didn't recognize.

"Yes," he answered, expecting a sales pitch.

"My name is Maude Abrams. I'm April Spencer's pediatrician."

Kurt stopped with his shoe in hand. April *Spencer*? As in *Stuart Spencer*? It hadn't occurred to him that Carol was presenting April as the other man's child.

And yet it wasn't out of character. "Her legal name is April Reynolds," he informed the woman tightly.

"Ah, yes, it would be, wouldn't it," she answered without any emotion registering in her voice. "I'm calling in regards to April's fear of strangers."

Kurt finally put his shoe on the floor. "What can I do for you?"

"April's mother has discussed with me the fact that your visits exacerbate the child's phobia. She's also told me you refuse to give them up. Mrs. Spencer asked that I speak to you."

"So you're a doctor," Kurt said contemplatively.

"Yes."

"But I have only your word for that."

"Yes," she allowed. "At the moment. But you could check it out for yourself."

"Uh-huh. And you're being paid by my ex-wife to tell me to stay away from my daughter."

"I'm being paid by Carol Spencer to treat April. That involves whatever is best for the child."

"Is that right? And Carol dictates what you should say is best for April, no doubt."

Silence. Kurt let it lapse until his frustration level broke. "All right, let's have it. Why are you calling?" he demanded none too friendly.

"Merely to confirm for you how serious April's fear has become, and to tell you that I think some alterations in the present situation might be in her best interest."

"One alteration being that I no longer see her."

"Of course that would be up to you. But should you put a moratorium on your visits until April has conquered this fear—"

"Which Carol can conveniently claim never happens," he interrupted.

"And then re-introduce yourself slowly, I think it might remove a certain amount of tension from her. That can only help her get over this."

"And I think it's likely that you don't have anything to back that up, certainly not professional credentials. I'd say there's a fifty-fifty chance that all you are is one of Carol's friends doing her a favor. So if you'll excuse me, I'm going to hang up."

He did just that. For a moment Kurt sat staring into space. Anger, frustration and guilt rolled through him. What if the woman had been who and what she said she was? What if he really was doing April harm by forcing himself on her?

Kurt threw his shoes hard enough to dent the closet wall.

There was one thing he admitted to himself. If he was absolutely sure that he wasn't harming April by seeing her, he wouldn't have gotten so damn mad.

Gillie was waiting with the door open when Kurt got there. She had been listening for his car. "I hope you came hungry, Reynolds, because the third member of our party threw us over for an extraterrestrial," she said as he came in.

His smile seemed a little late. "One landed in your backyard and took him off to another planet for study of boys who put salt in vanilla pudding?"

Gillie grimaced. "Told you about that one, did he?"

Kurt caught Gillie at the waist and pulled her in for a kiss that lasted longer than mere greeting called for. When his lips left hers, he sighed, pressed her cheek against his chest and settled his chin atop her head. "So where is our third party really?"

Gillie could hear his heart beating faster than usual. She might have been flattered except that she sensed a tension in him that somehow didn't feel sexual. "His friend Matt invited him for dinner and to watch a movie about an extraterrestrial on video tape. Since they promised to have him home by bedtime I gave in."

Kurt didn't respond right away. Then he said, "I'm sorry, my mind is out in the ozone somewhere. Where did you say Elijah was?"

Gillie repeated what she'd said, and added, "And I have a huge roast in the oven so I hope you're hungry."

"Damn." He let go of her and hit his forehead with the heel of his hand. "I forgot dessert. I'll go back."

"It's not important. Forget it. Elijah's not here to complain and I certainly don't need it."

"You're sure? I don't mind going home to get it."

The deep concern in his expression made her smile and frown at the same time. "It's no big deal. Want a glass of wine before dinner?"

"To tell you the truth, I'd like a stiff Scotch. Any chance of that?"

"Sure," she answered, looking a little closer at him. He didn't seem as if he was all there tonight. She took a small bottle of liquor from the cupboard beneath one of the end tables and headed to the kitchen with it. "Are you okay?"

He didn't follow her and that alone was unusual. From the living room he called, "No, I'm not."

"Want this over ice, not over ice, diluted?" she asked as if she hadn't heard, her stomach turned to instant knots. She was glad their talk on Sunday night hadn't gone any further and suddenly worried that it was something about their relationship that was what was troubling him—a difficult subject for her to discuss.

"Undiluted and over ice," he answered her.

Gillie could hear him pacing and knew she couldn't avoid discussing something that had him this uneasy. She took a breath and, hoping her reluctance was hidden, said, "Dinner can wait a while if you want to talk."

"Good, because right now I don't have an appetite," he told her as she came back into the living room and handed him his drink. He took a long pull of the Scotch, then informed her, "A woman claiming to be April's pediatrician called me a little while ago."

Gillie perched on the arm of the recliner and watched him pace. As long as it wasn't love or feelings or their relationship that was troubling him she could be an impartial listener, a role much easier on the nerves. "*Claiming* to be?"

But he seemed lost in his own thoughts and didn't hear her question. "Maude Abrams. Supposedly the pediatrician of April *Spencer*. Not April Reynolds."

Gillie flinched for how that must have made him feel. "What did the woman want?" she tried again to penetrate his thoughts and get a grip on what had happened.

After a moment Kurt related the call to her. "So now I have a professional's opinion that I should stay away from my daughter. If she really is a professional."

"Who do you think she might be?"

"One of Carol's friends probably. My ex-wife would do anything to get what she wants."

His marriage, especially the end of it, was something Gillie had an unsatisfied curiosity about. They had discussed his daughter and his ex-wife's pretentious bent, but he hadn't offered much information beyond that. It had been on Gillie's mind more and more, and now made her wonder if the woman had some reason for what seemed vindictive to Gillie.

"We've talked a lot about how you see your role in Elijah's life, about your daughter and what's happening with her—all the child-related stuff. But you've never told me the reason your marriage ended," she ventured.

"What has that got to do with anything?" He stopped pacing and pierced her with troubled green eyes.

Gillie shrugged and opted for honesty. "Why does she want to hurt you like this?"

He finished his Scotch, went into the kitchen and came back with his glass half full. "It isn't that she wants to hurt me. She couldn't care less about hurting me, in fact. I told you before that this is all to keep her skeleton in the closet. She's obviously gone so far as to pass April off as Stuart's daughter. She just wants the shadow of a failed marriage out of her picture postcard.''

He went back to pacing and Gillie thought she wasn't going to get an answer to her question about what had destroyed his marriage. Then he sighed and said, ''This is where you learn that I still have some remnants of that macho mentality I told you about before.''

''I don't understand,'' she said carefully, watching him as he went to the wall that displayed her family photographs, steadfastly not meeting her eyes.

''Through all of your husband's problems, was he faithful to you?''

This time it was Gillie who let silence lapse for a beat. ''I don't know. Or as far as I know he was. But—'' She sighed and felt tension tie her stomach again. ''There were long periods of time when I didn't know where he was. He could have been doing anything then.''

''But it wasn't as if you ever knew for sure.''

''No,'' she admitted, hearing a tinge of relief in her own voice. There had been enough to contend with without that, too.

''When cheating destroys a marriage it isn't something a person is anxious to announce. Especially a man. There's a real blow to your ego...even when you know what's really behind it doesn't have much to do with you personally.'' Another sip of his drink and he went on.

"When I met Carol I was a big man on campus. It didn't occur to me that she didn't want me for the person I am, but for the status I brought with me. We were married before I came to that crossroads I told you about, where I chose between a pro football career or going on with my schooling. Turning my back on professional sports brought me face-to-face with a big difference in what Carol wanted and what I wanted. She had counted on being the wife of a football celebrity, complete with all the trappings those millions could buy. Being stuck with a teacher-night-school student who barely earned enough for our small apartment did not please her."

"Didn't you realize before what she wanted out of life?"

He shrugged. "The signs were there but I chose not to see them. I loved her, but more than that I didn't want to see anything that would stop me from finally having what I'd wanted for as long as I can remember, what I'd missed as a kid—a family of my own. I figured we'd get married, buy a house, fill it with kids, noise, commotion, chaos and clutter. Marrying Carol, who came from just that sort of background, seemed like the first step."

"But she stayed with you even though you turned the football career down," Gillie prompted.

He took a breath that swelled his chest before answering. "Things were rocky between us for a long time. Then, when I told her I was going for my Ph.D. she perked up. Though I didn't realize it at the time, she pictured me as the head of some giant corporation. She was sure that once I'd finished all that schooling I was not going to be satisfied in the field of education. As she told me when we argued about my taking the job as headmaster of Lancaster, she wanted to be one of the prominent parents of children who *attended* the school, not the wife of a man working *for* those parents. She threatened then to leave if I didn't raise myself up to where I belonged, but before she could go through with it she found out she was pregnant."

He took another pull of his drink. "I half expected her to use the baby as a wedge, to give me the ultimatum that if I wanted to keep my family I'd have to alter my career to suit her. But she didn't even bother. She met Stuart a few weeks after April was born and I don't think she even hesitated to hop into bed with him. By the time April was six months old we were divorced."

Gillie breathed a silent sigh. Then it was all true—his ex-wife was the villain of the piece, her villainy just continuing on now. There was nothing wrong with Kurt as a man or husband any more than there was anything wrong with him as a father or in his relationships with kids. Gillie went back to the matter at hand with a feeling of great relief.

"Would it be a deciding factor in whether or not you went on seeing your daughter if you knew for sure that the woman who called you was a doctor?"

He thought about that. Then he shook his head. "If I was considering not seeing April anymore it might be an influencing factor, but not a deciding one."

Gillie gauged her words. She was treading on shaky ground and she knew it. "I think you are considering it," she said quietly.

He didn't say anything. He didn't look her way.

Gillie went on gently. "If you weren't considering that the best thing for April might be for you not to see her anymore, the whole thing wouldn't be on your mind so much. You wouldn't be as upset over a phone call like that. I think...I think that somewhere in your head you're weighing whether or not it is best for April if you do bow out."

Still he didn't say a word. His silence went on for so long that she began to wonder if he was too furious with her to speak. Then he sighed. He dropped his head forward and rubbed the back of his neck.

"You're right. Somewhere in my mind I guess that's just what I've been considering. Only it hurts too much to think about it up front." He finally looked at her. "But I think it's time I face it."

"I have a suggestion," she offered tentatively.

"I'm open for one."

"Talk to a psychologist."

"Now you think I've gone nuts?"

"Not for yourself—although I don't think you have to be nuts to need some counseling—but about April. Get some professional advice to combat this and to help you with your decision. Getting a big brother for Lijah was the school psychologist's idea, something I had never thought of before. Sometimes an objective perspective that comes out of that particular education and experience can really help. At least you might come away with an inkling of what's best for April, of whether you really should leave her alone or keep forcing the issue.''

Kurt thought about that for a moment, staring down into his drink. Then he raised his eyes to her and smiled, slowly, appreciatively. ''You're a smart lady, do you know that?''

''Good as the radio shrink?'' she joked, because it was obvious he felt a certain amount of relief in the idea.

Kurt came to stand directly in front of her. He laid his arms on her shoulders and leaned down to stare into her eyes, nose-to-nose. ''Thanks,'' he said, sounding like himself for the first time since he had arrived. ''I've been reading everything I can get my hands on about kids but nothing deals with this particular situation so it hasn't been much help. But I think this has distinct possibilities.'' He took a deep breath and sighed it out, smiling his most winning smile. ''This is probably going to sound crazy to you.'' He rubbed her nose with his. ''But just having a plan makes me feel better. And what I want right now, more than anything, is to make love to you and forget everything and everyone else in the world.''

Gillie smiled, relieved that nothing ugly had been revealed to her, relieved that he hadn't reacted to what she had said with anger, and pleased at having been able to help him. ''If I'm not mistaken, we have a good hour or two before the invasion of the extraterrestrials is over.''

''I like my roast beef well done, how about you?''

Gillie smiled innocently. ''What roast beef?''

He laughed just a little, a sensuous sound, and bent to kiss her, first tugging her upper lip between his and then her lower. Standing straight again, he smiled lazily down at her, telling her with the intensity of those gorgeous green eyes just how much he wanted her, just how much he appreciated her in every way.

The Scotch glass went to the end table, and Kurt led Gillie to her bedroom.

He turned on the bedside lamp, which cast a pale light in the room, before turning his attention to undressing Gillie. She didn't feel embarrassed by not being in the dark tonight and she wondered if that was because he had let her see the part of him and his history that had been missing from her knowledge. It seemed to take away the last of her own inhibitions.

She undressed him as freely, and together they lay on the bed, reveling in the wonder of that first touch of bare flesh to bare flesh. He held her tightly against him, one leg wrapped around her to keep her there as his mouth found hers in a leisurely beginning. His tongue courted and teased and Gillie's played the same game. His hand slid down her back, squeezed her rear, then trailed fire up her side to her breast, which his palm covered completely, setting off waves of undulating pleasure all through her.

There was a blending of newness and familiarity that left them relaxed and yet still curious. Gillie traced the curve of his ear with her tongue, nipped his lobe and laughed when he shuddered with the sensation. Then she licked a path down his jawline to his chin.

With a low moan of sensual challenge accepted, Kurt turned her onto her stomach and began to nibble the back of her neck as his hands worked her braid free and his fingers combed through her hair. Then he kissed his way down, tracing each shoulder blade and following the indentation of her spine with his tongue. He again found that sensitive spot on her side.

As desire grew in her, playfulness subsided and she rolled onto her back. With palms flattened against his muscular back Gillie drew him up and met his mouth with her own, open and seeking. He chuckled knowingly and again found her breast with his hand, kneading firmly, tracing her nipple round and round with just the knuckle of his thumb before rolling it gently.

When he dropped down and took that already straining crest in his mouth Gillie's back arched on its own and part groan, part sigh came out on a breath. She succumbed to the wonderful, warm, wet sensations until his hand reached lower and electric charges went off to replace languorous enjoyment with rapidly building need.

His fingers were magic, flicking, fluttering, plunging in and coming out again to slide forward and drive her wild. Gillie took him between her hands, doing a little rolling and sliding of her own until his need was as strong as hers.

He came into her without hesitation, and her body molded around him in perfect fit. Together they found the beat and the pace, seeking, thrusting, riding waves of charged sensations until almost simultaneously they peaked. Clinging hard, they melded into one.

Kurt drew breath as if he hadn't before, and said in a raspy voice, "I love you, Gillie. So much."

The lid on her own feelings had been knocked off completely. Gillie felt reborn and free. Suddenly she knew with certainty that her feelings for this man were good and right. She felt safe. Finding out the real reasons for his divorce seemed to put to rest her last doubt. She could see no glimmer of anything lurking behind the surface. The answering words found Gillie's voice as naturally as what they had just shared. "I love you, too, Kurt."

For a long moment neither of them moved, neither of them spoke. They stayed holding one another, their bodies united, hollow to curve, hardness against softness.

Then Kurt left her, rolling to his back and pulling her up against his side, her cheek against his chest. "I want to hear it again."

Gillie watched her hand where it rested on the hard rise of his pectoral, running a finger through the coarse hair there that matched the dark walnut on his head. "Don't you believe me?" she teased.

"I want to know you meant it."

"I meant it. I do love you, Kurt."

"Then what are we going to do about it?"

Gillie craned her head back to look up into his face. He was very solemn. "Do we have to do anything about it?"

"Of course we have to do something about it. I think we should get married."

Gillie shivered.

Kurt covered them with the bedspread and held her tighter. Then he went on before she could say anything. "I want you to be my wife, Gillie. I want Elijah to be my son. What I don't want is the three of us apart. Or you and I walking on eggs trying not to let him see just how we feel about each other. Or only being able to make love to you or spend the night with you when he's gone so he doesn't catch on to what we're doing. I don't think you want any of those things, either, do you?"

"No," she answered him honestly. "But…anything else seems so…soon."

He ran his hand from her waist to her shoulder. "We're good together, Gillie. Not only in bed, but outside of it, too. Tonight is a prime example of how we balance each other, of how we see perspectives the other misses, of how we complement and complete each other."

There was no arguing what he said because she knew it was all true. But another doubt niggled. "I know a family is what you want more than anything in the world. I wouldn't like to think that Elijah and I—"

"Were a package deal to fulfill that fantasy?" he finished for her. "If that was what I wanted do you think I couldn't have had it a dozen times over since my divorce. Unfortunately there are all too many of them out there, just waiting to be plucked by anyone so inclined. It isn't a family I want to marry. It's you, Gillie."

"I just don't know…" She really didn't. A part of her wanted to give in, to accept him and the love they shared, however new it was, and believe in happily ever after. But there was another part of her that had been saying no to that belief for too long to be completely at ease so quickly.

"Why don't you know, Gillie?" His voice was very deep, still husky from lovemaking.

"It scares me," she admitted with a strength in her tone that told him just how much. "You can't tell me that after what you've been through the thought of marriage the second time around doesn't give you cause for alarm."

There was a solemn confidence in his voice. "Our getting married isn't something I've come to on the spur of the moment, if that's how it seems to you. I've thought a lot about it. Loving you makes me vulnerable and being vulnerable to someone again scares the hell out of me, too. But there it is, Gillie. And every instinct I have is telling me to ignore the fear and go for it. You can't let the fear rule."

For a moment he paused, his hand still gently rubbing her back. "I've played it safe for two and a half years, Gil. Or at least that's what I thought I was doing. Now it seems as if that cool, aloof, keep-myself-removed stuff wasn't by choice. I only accomplished it because I hadn't met a woman who made me feel the way you do, the things I feel when I'm with you and not with you. Now I couldn't be cool or aloof or removed if my life depended on it. I didn't even feel this way with Carol, try that one on if you want to feel some high grade fear of vulnerability. But here it all is and I don't think either of us could or should let it slip away, no matter how frightening it is."

Gillie sat up in bed, pulling the blanket like a shawl around herself. She propped her chin on an upraised knee.

"Think about it," he suggested tenderly. "And then give me an answer."

There wasn't a way to think about anything else.

Kurt sat up and swung off the bed. "If I stay here I'm not going to be able to keep from pleading my case. So I'm going to leave and give you some space."

Gillie didn't want him to go and yet she did need time alone to think about this. "I invited you for dinner and then send you home hungry."

He grinned at her over his shoulder as he pulled on his pants. "You're right. Hungry for a whole life with you." He winked at her and added, "If a little guilt will help my cause I'm not above it." He tossed her clothes at her. "Get dressed and walk me to the door. Lijah'll be home any minute and you can't meet him in your bathrobe—one more of those little nuisances we could avoid by making this legal."

Gillie rolled her eyes at him in mock irritation.

"See why I have to go? I can find a million reasons to convince you. But I want the only one to be that you love me."

Minutes later when they were both dressed and Gillie had even braided her hair again, Kurt wrapped her in his arms at the front door.

"I love you, Hunter," he said so sincerely it expanded her heart like a balloon.

"I love you, too, Reynolds," she whispered back, in awe of the weight of her own feelings for him now that they were free.

He kissed her, long and deep, then let her go. "I'll talk to you tomorrow."

Even the frigid gust of air that washed over Gillie when he opened the door didn't penetrate her preoccupied thoughts. She watched him drive away, closed the door and leaned against it.

If only there was something or someone to let her see the future and know it was all right to let this happen again.

She heard a car pull into the drive. Assuming it was Elijah coming home made her consider what it would mean to have Kurt for a stepfather. Only good things came to mind.

The doorbell rang and she turned to answer it, her head spinning with a million different thoughts.

But it wasn't Elijah on the other side of that door.

Gillie couldn't believe what she was seeing. She closed her eyes for a moment, as if that would clear her vision. When she opened them again she looked out to the big, black beat-up car in her driveway before raising her glance to the man standing before her.

"I should have put two and two together but it's been so long. You're Elijah's do-gooding elves, aren't you?"

Chapter Ten

The worst cold snap in Colorado's history has settled in just as predicted.''

Kurt brought his second cup of coffee into the living room as the radio heralded the Friday morning weather report. Kurt had taken the day off to catch the only flight out of Denver for Connecticut and was generally feeling pretty good about everything.

After he'd left Gillie the night before, the thought of contacting a child psychologist to discuss the best course for his and April's relationship had been on his mind. So much so, that he had taken out the phone book to see what sort of services were available in hopes that he might be able to contact someone this morning before he left. He had found a twenty-four-hour help line number for the psychiatric ward of

Denver's Children's Hospital. A long conversation with the doctor who answered had left him with a clear idea of what was the best course for his daughter. He'd decided to allow himself one last chance this weekend for her birthday, but if the situation was unchanged, he knew what he had to do from there.

And then there was Gillie.

He believed she was going to accept his proposal. He couldn't think of a reason she wouldn't. He loved her, she loved him, they were great together, he and Elijah were great together, the three of them were great together—what more could anyone want? Between sips of coffee, he whistled as he dressed.

Gillie would think things over, realize getting married was just the next step in the natural order of things, the best choice for them all, and that would be that. He even had high hopes that his visit with his daughter would prove different than usual.

"If Gillie doesn't want a big wedding we may even be able to have it done in time to be a family for Christmas," he told his reflection in the mirror as he shaved.

The thought of leaving at noon and not seeing her for three days was an unpleasant one, so Kurt decided to make the most of the few hours before he had to be at the airport. With any luck she would have already made up her mind and an impromptu breakfast date would serve as a celebration.

Kurt drove slightly over the speed limit on the way to her house, hoping he'd get there before she left to take Elijah to school and they could do it together. But he was a little late for that; he met Bob Baumgardner with Elijah in a car at the stop sign at the end of Gillie's street.

Kurt pulled up alongside and rolled down his window, wondering why his friend was frowning and Elijah looked as glum.

"Morning, guys," Kurt called in a steamy cloud of his own breath.

"Morning," Bob answered, seeming uncomfortable.

"Where's Gillie this morning?" he asked. She had told him that unless it was an emergency she took Lijah to school herself so as not to impose on Bob and because it embarrassed her son to arrive with the principal.

"She's home." He glanced at his ten-year-old passenger, then back at Kurt. "Lijah spent the night with us so he and I are carpooling this morning."

Elijah had spent the night? That was odd. But before Kurt could ask any questions another car pulled up behind Bob.

"We'd better get going. We're holding up traffic," Bob said.

"Sure," Kurt agreed, confused. "Have a good day, Lijah."

His sense that something was up was only compounded when he got to Gillie's house and found a big, black, beat-up car parked in the driveway. Thinking of the solemn expressions on both Bob and Elijah's faces, he doubted that whatever was going on was good. Worry got him parked in the driveway and out of his own car in a hurry.

He rang the doorbell, then knocked, leaning to look in the window. He saw Gillie come from the kitchen to answer. She was dressed in her usual jeans and turtleneck, her hair braided, but she looked tired and drawn, and Kurt's worries peaked.

She opened the door and her expression relaxed. "You must have ESP," she breathed as she held the screen door for him to come in. "Just when I need a morale booster, here you are."

"I played hooky to come and whisk you off for breakfast," he explained, then didn't hesitate to add, "Is everything all right around here? I met Bob and Lijah at the corner. They didn't look too happy, and when I peeked through the window neither did you."

"It's a long story." She glanced over her shoulder a little nervously. "Breakfast was a nice thought, though, and I wish I could go, but I can't. Not this morning."

Kurt nodded over his shoulder at the black car and joked, "Have I caught you at something you shouldn't be doing?"

She laughed slightly and shook her head, but before she answered a male voice said, "Gil, there's no soap in the shower." A man appeared from the hallway wearing only a towel wrapped around his waist.

Kurt's glance went from Gillie to the nearly naked man and back again. Her face blanched, making the dark circles under her eyes all the more noticeable.

"Kurt," she began in a voice so soft she needed to stop and clear her throat before going on. "This is my ex-husband, Phil Hunter."

Phil's expression went from curious to angry before Gillie had even completed the introduction and Kurt had a sudden flash of memory that his neighbor had claimed the car that had rammed his Volvo on Thanksgiving had been big, black, and beat-up. He looked at the one out front and found the rear fender crumpled.

"I think we need to talk," Kurt said to Gillie, trying to keep his voice emotionless when he was feeling anything but.

"I thought you were going to fix me some breakfast," Phil reminded with an almost whining undertone to his voice.

Gillie answered him in the conciliating way she might have Elijah. "There's another bar of soap in the medicine cabinet and the only thing around here for breakfast is cereal. Why don't you take your shower first?"

Kurt watched the other man stare expectantly at Gillie. His hair was long, nearly to his shoulders, and his face was as overgrown with beard and mustache as an empty lot is with weeds.

When Phil didn't respond to her suggestion, Gillie went on. "Kurt and I are going to go for a walk. I'll be back in a little while." She rushed out ahead of Kurt, holding the screen door for him to follow.

He threw a glare the other man's way and pulled the door closed after himself. "You don't even have a coat on," he said tightly.

"I'll be okay."

He took her hand and pulled her down the porch steps. "No, you won't be okay." He opened the passenger side of the Volvo and pressed her into it.

"I can't leave," she told him quickly.

"We don't have to go anywhere to run the heater." As he rounded the car, Kurt tried to keep a grip on the instant anger that had come with the sight of another man—in a towel—in Gillie's house. He only managed a tenuous hold by the time he got in behind the wheel and started both the engine and the heater. Then he turned toward her. "Now tell me what the hell is going on."

Gillie sighed, shook her head and looked at him. "He smashed your car," she admitted what he had surmised for himself already. "I'm sorry."

"What are you sorry for? You aren't responsible. But why the hell is he in your house? Why the hell is he in your life again, for that matter?"

She looked straight ahead at the garage door. "It's so complicated," she said wearily.

"Did he show up here this morning?"

She shook her head. "Last night right after you left. I should have seen it coming, all the signs were there, but—"

"You've lost me."

"I told you he would disappear for months. Well, autumn was always a prime time for him to come home. He was usually living out of his car and with the cold weather... Anyway, he would sort of lurk around before he actually came to face me. This time was typical. My leaves were raked in the middle of the night, only I thought it was part of a deal I had made with Danny Baumgardner. I guess Phil has been parking out front a lot, trying to get up the nerve to come to the door. Remember the blizzard when you spent the day with Elijah and me? There were tire tracks in my driveway from the night before that I thought were suspicious, but then I figured I was just paranoid. Later, in that bad windstorm we had over Thanksgiving weekend, he was parked out front then, too and when the gate blew open he closed it, bent the latch and used some motor oil on the hinges. I thought my neighbor had done that one. And he ran into your car," she repeated sheepishly. "I guess he'd been watching enough to know we were getting closer and closer."

"And he didn't want me invading territory he was about to move back into," Kurt finished disgustedly. "I thought you were divorced from this guy."

"I am."

"Then what does he want?"

She rubbed her temple as if she had a headache. "My help. He wants to get clean, put himself into an outpatient rehabilitation program to get off the drugs and alcohol, finally deal with his posttraumatic stress disorder from Vietnam."

"Commendable," Kurt clipped. "But why outpatient and what does he need you for?"

"He doesn't want to be committed to a hospital. Feeling locked up is one of the things that bothers him."

She hadn't answered the other part of his question. Kurt guessed with the full measure of the distaste he felt ringing in his voice. "And he wants you to take him in, hold his hand and support him through it."

She swallowed visibly. "Yes."

"Of course you told him no."

The only sound in the car was the whir of the heater.

"Gillie? You did tell him you wouldn't take him in, didn't you?" But then she already *had* taken him in, Kurt realized suddenly. Emphatically he repeated, "Didn't you?" when she still didn't answer.

"I haven't told him anything yet. I said I have to think about it," she finally admitted.

Kurt raised his eyebrows and closed his eyes for a moment, searching for patience he didn't feel. Then he said, "What is there to think about?"

"It isn't as cut and dried as it might look to you," she hedged.

"You're right, it looks pretty cut and dried to me. You divorced the man because he had delayed stress that he dealt with by drinking, taking drugs and disappearing. If I had to put money on it I'd bet that every time he showed up back here it was with a variation of this story about wanting to clean up his act. You'd give him the chance, let him come home, he'd tow the mark for a while—mostly through the worst of the winter—and then as spring returned so did the evidence that he was back to his destructive behavior and he'd disappear again."

She nodded. "That's about it."

"If you finally came to the realization that he was lying and divorced him to break the cycle in your own life, why buy back into it now?"

"Because this time I think he's serious about getting help. Before he would make promises not to do the drugs and alcohol, not to disappear, but he wouldn't even listen to the idea of getting professional help. He would always say he could do it on his own, that it wasn't as if he couldn't stop the drugs or the liquor when he'd made up his mind to. But now he isn't making promises. He knows he can't shake either addiction without medical care, counseling and guidance. All he's asking of me is to support him while he does get professional help."

"*All* he's asking?"

"And I owe him," she finished so softly that Kurt barely heard her over the heater. She'd dropped her chin and sat staring at her knees, which bounced up and down in a nervous tremor.

"What could you possibly owe him?"

She turned away from him. When she finally answered, her voice seemed so far away he could barely hear her.

"It's all so complicated." Her braid swayed back and forth as she shook her head. "A long time ago I was engaged to a man named Paul North. I met him just before I finished art school. He was the son of a woman who played bridge with my mother."

"In California?"

"In California. He was tall, good-looking, smart. I was crazy about him and he said he was crazy about me. Girl meets boy, falls in love, he sweeps her off her feet and they live happily ever after. We were engaged within two months." She swung around to look at him finally, but couldn't seem to maintain eye contact as she went on. "Paul was an electrical engineer. Just after we got engaged he was offered a job in Colorado. He said he was glad that he'd have me to move out here with, that he wouldn't be coming alone, that I had family already here. We were to be married as soon as we were settled. He gave the impression of being very decisive, of knowing exactly what he wanted. He went on and on about how much he loved me, how much he wanted to get married, how perfect we were together. He had me convinced. He had my whole family convinced. So, I jumped right in with both feet. Paul got an apartment, I moved in with Robin and Bob, and started reading cookbooks, planning a wedding in a mountain chapel and looking for a little job that would help out financially." She rolled her eyes. "Lord, but I was dumb to think that working was just a lark for a woman and making a living was what men did."

"And?" Kurt prompted.

"I got pregnant a little ahead of schedule."

A ripple of shock ran through him.

"Blink, Kurt, before your eyeballs dry out."

"Elijah?" was all he could manage to get into words.

She nodded. "Just when you think you know someone... I told Paul about the baby. I knew it would be a shock. It was a shock to me. But rather than just moving the wedding date up, which was what I expected, he told me he'd had second thoughts. He said he didn't think he was ready to settle down after all. And then he was gone. Poof! Up in smoke. All of a sudden being a temporary houseguest turned into being a charity case. I was unemployed, pregnant and . . . lost. Having an abortion was just something I couldn't do. I couldn't go back home to my folks, I was a late-life baby myself and they were too far along in years to end up with an unwed, pregnant daughter on their doorstep. I was so sick I couldn't even go out looking for a job, let alone make it to work every day if I had found one, and I just plain didn't know what to do.''

Kurt watched her eyes fill with tears as if she were reliving the past, but she didn't cry. She looked straight ahead again and waited for her eyes to dry before she went on.

"I was so scared. I can't begin to tell you how much," she said, her voice soft. "Until Phil came around. Bob and Robin hired him to build an addition onto their house. He had been back from Vietnam for two years and he seemed like the nicest man I had ever known. I'm sure at first he just felt sorry for me—Robin had filled him in, she's always been pretty free with her stories. I've told you he got me my first ad art job. It was something I could do at home, so I could work around the morning sickness. Then he started getting me out of the house, taking me on walks, doing things that were good for me physically and mentally, thoughtful things. Step by step he showed me how to go on. I loved him for that. When he said he wanted to marry me and be the father of my baby I really thought he was the silver lining in the cloud that had settled over my life. We were married two weeks before Elijah was born and I did a lot of counting my blessings.''

"So Phil is Lijah's father legally but not his biological one," he clarified for himself.

"Better than a soap opera, isn't it?" she said ruefully.

"Does Lijah know?"

Gillie dropped her head back and stared up at the car roof. "No. How could I explain something so convoluted to him? When he's older I will, of course, but not until I think he'll be able to understand."

"And you didn't have any idea about Phil's problems until after you were married?"

"No. But right afterward I realized he could be very moody and he had nightmares, terrible, terrible, nightmares. For a while he was functioning. It wasn't until later that I learned that was the pattern—his drinking would slow down enough to give the appearance of his leading a normal life. That's what was going on when we met. But he couldn't sustain it. That first time around it lasted long enough for us to buy this house, to start settling into married life, then his experiences in Vietnam resurfaced to haunt him. In those days delayed stress wasn't something that was openly discussed the way it is now. At least I didn't know anything about it and he didn't really understand it himself." Gillie took a breath.

"Little by little during that first year we were married his moodiness turned into a deep depression. The fact that Elijah was a boy seemed to eat at him. Phil became obsessed with thoughts about Lijah góing off to war. The drinking I thought was only social because he had hidden the worst of it became constant. He said it was the only way to escape the flashbacks and the nightmares. By the time we had been married a little over a year, Phil was taking drugs on top of it. He couldn't hold a job, he was in a rage most of the time so if his inability to function properly didn't get him fired his temper did. Then one night we had a bad argument and he walked out. I didn't hear from him or know where he was for two months. After that . . . well, you know the rest.''

"So that's why it had been eight years since—"

"Before he took off our life was not filled with marital bliss. He was in and out, drunk or drugged. I had more pride than to sleep with him when he did show up," she admitted softly. "When he came back that last time I told him I had to get a divorce, that I couldn't take it anymore. He stayed in contact until the divorce was final and then I just didn't see him or hear from him again.''

"And what do you think you owe him now?" he asked her, his own doubts about that echoing.

She flashed a quick frown his way. "Haven't you heard what I've been saying? He helped me when I needed it, he gave me dignity at a time when it had all been taken away. Now that's what he's asking of me. He needs my help the same way I used his and he wants to be able to get back on his feet with the same dignity he allowed me. I owe him that.''

"What he wants is a warm place to come in out of the cold again just like before and he's using anything he thinks will work to accomplish it," Kurt said before he'd thought about whether or not it was wise to be so blunt.

She looked at him as if she'd just spotted green scales on his skin. "You don't know that. You don't know anything about him."

"I know I don't like him in your house, or anywhere near you or Elijah. I know I don't want him in our life together."

"What do you want me to do? Throw him out? Say, 'Tough luck, I can't be bothered with your problems now that I'm on the verge of some good times'?"

All Kurt could see in his mind's eye was a half-naked man acting as if he owned her. "The guy is a drug addict, an alcoholic. He purposely rams into other people's cars because he doesn't like what's going on. This is not a rational person, to say the least, Gillie. For all you know he's been in jail or institutionalized for the last five years and that's why you haven't seen him."

"He's a sick man, a person with a lot of problems, but he isn't a criminal. He wouldn't hurt me or Elijah," she shouted suddenly.

"Then why did you have Lijah spend the night at the Baumgardners'?"

That seemed to knock the wind out of her sails but still she defended, "Phil looked bad. I didn't want Elijah frightened."

"And you think a shower and a shave is all it's going to take to fix that? I think any contact with this guy is pretty frightening."

"You're condemning him because of the way he looks," she accused. "I gave you credit for more than that. Yes, his appearance is unsavory. Yes, he's probably lived a pretty unsavory life for the past five years—''

"And before, when he was going in and out of your house," Kurt cut in pointedly.

Gillie ignored it. "And yes, he has some unsavory problems. But underneath all of that is a man who nearly saved my life. A man who gave Elijah a name and made it possible for me to support my child, to keep a roof over his head and raise him. And that's the man I owe, for my sake and for Elijah's. I have my doubts about how much I can help him, or even if I can at all, but I know him well enough to know there is no danger in being around him."

"Do you?"

"Yes, I do. I didn't know what was under the surface when I married him, but I've seen his true colors since, believe me."

"Have you? Or are you just overlooking the truth because you still love him?" he demanded then.

"Love him?" she repeated incredulously. Then she rolled her eyes again in exasperation. "I care for him, yes, but no, I don't love him, not the way you mean."

Somehow to hear that she cared for him at all rubbed Kurt the wrong way. "So what are you going to do? How far will you go to pay back your debt?"

"I don't know," she said morosely. Her whole face was puckered into a frown as she looked away, continuing in a soft tone, "I won't let him stay here. I was going to tell him that much after his breakfast. It isn't that I think Phil would hurt him, but I don't want Elijah around this sort of thing."

Kurt was glad to see she was thinking straight enough to realize that if nothing else. "Neither one of you should be around this sort of thing. His problems are his own, Gillie."

"And my problems ten years ago were my own. Are you really the kind of person who takes for himself what he needs and then turns his back on that debt when it comes time to repay it? People volunteer to help strangers with their problems. They donate money to organizations that provide housing or food or rehabilitation. You yourself suggested to your student council that they collect clothes and blankets to donate to the homeless. Is it only something to do from a distance? As long as you don't dirty your hands? What Phil is asking is the same kind of aid, only he's asking it of me, the only person in the world who actually does owe it to him. Why is it so hard for you see that?"

"What it's hard—no, impossible for me to see is why you'd buy his bill of goods unless you *care* a lot more about him than you're admitting to either of us."

"And what I see—for the first time—is someone without understanding or compassion. Someone who is unreasonable and selfish enough to figure the taking is okay and the giving back can be reasoned out of."

"Or maybe you're just reasoning his way back into your life. I don't know why you'd want to, but hey, I'm certainly the last dumb jerk in the world to understand why a woman wants to juggle men."

"Juggle men?" she repeated, drawing up in outrage. "I can't believe— Now you're not only suspicious of him but of me, too?"

He was, he admitted to himself, unable to get the picture of Phil Hunter wrapped in a towel coming out of her hallway, or the familiarity in the man's voice that made him appear to be right at home. But to her, he said, "It seems to me that the score is even. You gave him five years of your life trying to help him with his problems. As far as I can see you're all paid up."

"Because that's how you want to see it. I have an obligation here. If you can't live with that, I'm sorry."

"You don't have an obligation," he countered, his anger getting the better of him. "You divorced him five years ago because you couldn't help him then and you can't now."

"Now that I have you and should be devoting myself to the happily-ever-after you're offering, is that it? And I should just forget my past, forget all he did for me."

"You should be realistic."

She pierced him with her eyes. "I think I am seeing things realistically for the first time. The bottom line here is that you refuse to understand that I honestly owe Phil. That you want to look at it as some ridiculous love affair. That you're unreasonable when I thought you might be my support through this."

"How can I be supportive of this guy's manipulative guilt trip? And no, I don't understand why you would even consider this, unless your feelings for him are unresolved. Why else would you rather put what we have in jeopardy?"

"I didn't realize I would be," she said in a tone more effective for its softness than its anger. "But then suddenly I'm seeing a lot of things I missed before. I don't think I'm too crazy about your opinions of me. And I'm not sure mine of you are too great right now, either." Belying her controlled tone, she flung open the car door and got out, slamming it after herself.

Kurt charged out of his side of the car and caught her by the arm as she headed toward the house. "Look," he tried to force patience. "I know you're under a strain right now—"

But that was as far as he got before she yanked her arm free. "That's right and I don't need anymore. I haven't thought a lot about this, but what I did think was that I had some backing from you. That no matter how tough or how unpleasant it might be to repay this debt, you would be understanding, that you would pitch in and help out with Elijah while I do whatever I have to with Phil, that you'd be generous, sympathetic and unequivocally supportive." Her eyes were full of disillusionment. "And instead you're intolerant, condemning, suspicious and you don't want the neat order of your life disturbed with something that's not too nice. You just aren't what I thought you were."

And then she left him standing out in the cold.

Chapter Eleven

It wasn't easy for Kurt to board his plane for Connecticut three hours later. His mood was grim. Throughout the flight he marveled at how fast things could change for the worse. But then it wasn't the first time in his life that an hour had altered a future he thought was certain and secure. Carol's announcement that she was divorcing him to marry Stuart had landed the same blow.

Only this time it felt even worse.

His relationship with Carol hadn't been a bed of roses, the way he had thought his and Gillie's was. He hadn't come face-to-face with Stuart until much later, and then the other man hadn't been strutting his stuff in a towel. There also hadn't been this damn level of worry compounding his feelings. Stuart was not the kind of person who could do Carol or April any harm.

But Phil Hunter? A drug addict and alcoholic? Kurt was torn between being outraged and hurt, and just plain scared of the fact that Gillie and Elijah were within arm's reach of someone like that.

Kurt was still stewing when he disembarked and caught a cab to his hotel. The first thing he did after he had checked in was call to try to set up dinner with April. But Carol wasn't having any of that and his daughter cried and even refused to speak to him on the phone. The conversation ended with his ex-wife cursorily telling him what time the party started the next day before hanging up.

So much for high hopes that this visit would be different. But at least he knew now how he was going to handle it, which was not something he could say about the situation with Gillie.

Carol and Stuart's new home was the portrait of a gentleman's farm. They had been living in a city when he had last visited in August and this party was to be both a celebration of April's birthday and a housewarming. Kurt drove his rental car across a wooden bridge that arched over a babbling brook, and headed up a short cobbled road lined with white rail fences behind which were three chestnut mares. The house was a sprawling Georgian three-story building, the driveway circling a fountain.

There were already a number of cars parked there by the time Kurt arrived. According to what Carol had said on the phone the night before, he was two hours early—two hours that he was to have alone with April. Or as alone as he could be in the house with Carol and Stuart hanging around. But obviously even that was too much for his ex-wife to tolerate; she had lied so that he would be robbed of even those two hours. It didn't help a mood that was still clouded with thoughts of Gillie and concerns for what he had left her to.

"Valet parking?" he mumbled to himself as a starch-stiff teenager stepped out of the arch designed a hundred and fifty years ago to shelter a footman waiting to help guests out of their carriages. "Good to see you're still as pretentious as ever, Carol," he said under his breath just before getting out and handing the boy his keys.

The butler who answered the door asked to see his invitation. Kurt laughed and walked past him, shaking his head. "She doesn't miss a trick."

The house was brimming with people and children. Kurt wondered fleetingly if one of the women there was Maude Abrams. He had checked the phone book for her name and found nothing, making him more sure than ever that the phone call had been bogus.

He spotted April in the center of the formal living room, sitting on her mother's lap, opening gifts. She was dressed in a navy-blue velvet dress with a white lace collar and white lace tights. Her dark walnut-colored hair was a mass of tiny curls all around her head and just seeing her made him smile. She was fragile-looking, doll-like.

A maid asked to take his gift but Kurt swung it out of her reach. "I'm her father," he told the young girl proudly, obviously confusing her. "I'll wait and give her this later, after everyone else is gone." To confirm his intentions he slipped the box behind one of two matching Louis XV chairs and took up a position standing outside the circle of people, feasting on the sight of his daughter.

"Hello, Kurt."

Kurt didn't need to turn to know the man who had just come up and greeted him was April's stepfather. "Stuart," he replied, never taking his eyes off his daughter.

"I expected you earlier."

That made Kurt give a disdainful laugh. "Carol said the party was at one so I came at eleven."

"Ah," was all Stuart answered.

Kurt spared him a glance out of the corner of his eye, wondering what Stuart's reaction was to machinations he obviously didn't know were going on. He was shorter than Kurt by two inches, broader by eight, and had a hairline that was gradually creeping to his crown. But his expression was blank.

"I'll be staying later so I can see April alone," Kurt informed his host. "And then I'll need to speak to you and Carol before I go."

"All right," Stuart said cordially enough as he moved off. "In the meantime make yourself at home."

In search of coffee, Kurt stepped around the crowd and went up two steps into the dining area. Twin swan ice sculptures made the centerpiece of the brunch table, one holding a bowl with plain punch for the children and the other gracefully cradling one with champagne. Kurt accepted only coffee and then posted himself at the top of the steps so that he had a clear view of April as she finished with her gifts.

He watched every move his daughter made with more than his usual interest. He loved the little girl so much it literally filled his chest and made it tight. His arms ached to scoop her up and twirl her around, to make her laugh, to cuddle her, to blow on her round cheeks. He felt a deep pain and regret that he couldn't, that they were a long way from even the kind of easy rapport he and Elijah shared.

As long as April was in Carol's lap she seemed happy enough, if not outgoing. The other adults were obviously aware of the child's fear and gave her a wide berth, though when one or two of them ventured a word to Carol, even from a distance, April cringed and clung to her mother.

Kurt couldn't help being angry at his ex-wife. Hypocrite, he thought. For the sake of her image Carol used April's phobia to drive him away, and yet for the sake of that same image she would submit the child to all of this. If either of them was going to put April's problems before what they wanted, it would never be Carol.

Tall, blonde and model-perfect Carol. His ex-wife hadn't lost her looks, he admitted, realizing at the same time that he was impervious to that fact.

Would it be different, he couldn't help but wonder, if Carol had encouraged April to think of him as her father from the start? He believed it would have been. In spite of the divorce and distance, his love for April, his wanting to be a part of her life, didn't seem like such a complicated thing if only Carol would have accepted it and let it take a natural course. But not Carol. She wanted him and his every connection with April wiped off the face of the earth so no one would ever know she had begun somewhere without butlers, maids and valet parking.

The photographer that milled around snapping pictures of the event encouraged Stuart to join April and Carol for a family picture and as Kurt watched his thoughts settled on Stuart.

Kurt had never been blind enough to believe Carol had been innocently swept off her feet by Stuart. He realized that in all probability it had been Carol who had pursued Stuart. But he hadn't ever been too fond of the man for the role he had played in the breakup of the marriage, either. And he resented Stuart's place in April's heart.

In April's heart. That thought struck a cord.

Why hadn't he thought that he resented Stuart's place in her *life*?

But he knew why as he watched Stuart and April together. The little girl's face lit up with a smile. She hugged him, she called him Daddy. Without even the prompting of the photographer, she happily kissed him on the cheek.

No knife could have hurt Kurt more than being witness to his daughter's affection for another man. And yet he realized that in some strange way he also appreciated that the other man was Stuart. Kurt had known enough stepparents to realize that there wasn't always a bond between them and the children they were raising. But Stuart's answering smile at April was genuine and as loving as if she were actually his daughter. He squatted down beside her and pulled her up onto his knee to receive and return her hug. It even looked as if his eyes might have filled a little when she had kissed him.

Kurt couldn't help but think about how he'd been feeling leaving Elijah and Gillie in the hands of Phil

Hunter. That was worse, he realized, than leaving someone he loved in the hands of someone who loved them back. As hard as it was to see what was between April and Stuart, as jealous as it made him, it would have been worse to see her stepfather reject her, hurt her, not respond to her affection.

For April's sake, Kurt was grateful for that.

It was after three by the time the last guest had left. Whether it was fatigue or Carol's hostile hovering or the fact that April was probably more familiar with the guests than Kurt, the child was more upset at seeing Kurt than she had been during the party. She clung to Stuart's leg, pleading with him to make the strange man go away and leave her alone. She didn't even care about the doll Kurt had brought her. She cowered at every attempt he made. She shrieked in terror when he bent down and tried to persuade her to come to him.

After half an hour April began to cry hysterically and Carol scooped her up into her arms as if saving her from a monster, declaring that it was time for her to take a nap. Cradling the curly head against her shoulder, she reiterated that it was heartless of Kurt to put April through this. Then she walked out and left Kurt alone in the living room with Stuart.

"Could you use a drink?" the other man offered amiably as they waited for Carol to come back.

"As a matter of fact, I could," Kurt answered, surprising himself by feeling a tinge of camaraderie with his host.

"Scotch?"

"Please."

Stuart poured two glasses and brought one to Kurt. "Sit down, why don't you? You've been standing since you got here."

Kurt did, taking one end of a brocade sofa while Stuart sat in a wing chair.

"This must all be very hard for you—April's fear, Carol's animosity," Stuart mused.

"You'll never know," Kurt, staring into his glass, muttered more to himself than to Stuart.

"It isn't easy for Carol, either, regardless of what you think. She suffers almost as much as April over April's fear."

"It didn't stop her from turning this place into a three-ring circus today."

"She never left April alone for a second," he countered in his wife's defense.

"You think that makes up for it? I don't. She wants me to completely remove myself from my daughter's life rather than put April through the tension of seeing me, yet she didn't deny herself this spectacle today. Somehow it seems to me that if she was genuinely concerned she'd at least make an attempt to be friendly to me, to show April that I'm not an ogre, to encourage her to relax. Instead she just injects more tension with her hostility." Kurt had lost his temper. It was out of place with this man who was being hospitable. But Stuart didn't seem to take offense.

"Admittedly she doesn't help matters. But that isn't going to change. You know Carol."

He knew Carol all right. He also knew he was going to have to go through with the decision he'd made before.

Carol came back into the room and perched on the arm of Stuart's chair. "I hope what you want to talk to us about is that you're getting out of our life."

Kurt shook his head. "I didn't come to fight with you, Carol. And I'm not getting out of your life. At least not permanently."

Carol opened her mouth to speak but Kurt cut her off. "I want April put into therapy with a child psychologist."

His ex-wife's face flushed red with anger. "My daughter is not crazy."

"I didn't say she was. But she needs help."

"What she needs is for you to leave her alone."

"I'm not going to do that. At least not indefinitely." Kurt glanced at Stuart, wondering what his response was, and found the other man's expression indiscernible. He went on anyway. "You can choose the therapist and I'll pay for it, no matter what it costs. I'll also keep in touch with whoever it is and I'm warning you up front, Carol, that if April isn't taken for the appointments or if you don't cooperate with everything suggested to help her, I'll come after you legally. But until the psychologist advises it, I won't come here and force April to see me. I'll wait for the go-ahead, and then I'll slowly start to reintroduce myself into her life. But make no mistake about it—I will be a part of her life."

Carol shot to her feet in outrage but before she could find the words she was sputtering for, Stuart's hand clasped around her wrist and stopped her. "Stuart!" she shrieked instead, yanking from his grip.

Kurt watched as Stuart scowled at her.

"Kurt's right. April needs help." Her husband's agreement with Kurt seemed to shake Carol more than anything.

"April is *my* daughter," the woman ground out through clenched teeth.

"She's *my* daughter, too," Kurt put in forcefully. "And whether you like it or not, whether it tarnishes your image or not, from here on in I'm going to have my rights to her."

For a moment Carol was dumbstruck with rage. Then she lashed out, "I hope it takes twenty years for her to get over this. I hope it breaks you financially and you *still* never get to see her."

"Stop it, Carol," Stuart said quietly.

But Kurt was undisturbed. He stood up and faced her. "You've pushed me as far as I'm going, Carol. You'll get April into counseling and you won't interfere or impede it in any way or I *will* sue you for custody. And when April's conquered this, I'll have what the court granted me in the beginning—I'll have April with me in Denver for the summers and for half of the holidays. And believe me when I say I don't give a damn whether you like it or not. Now, since I won't be seeing my daughter for some time, I want one more look at her before I go."

Carol took a step toward him, Kurt stayed his ground, and Stuart pulled Carol back. "Go on up," Stuart told him, nodding toward the stairs.

"Thanks," Kurt said to the last man on earth he would ever have expected support from. Then he went up to his daughter's room.

The three-year-old was asleep, one arm curved around the teddy bear he'd bought her when Carol had first taken her away, only the snowy white fur was grayed and matted and one ear was chewed off. It was so scrungy looking he marveled at the fact that Carol would have it in her house and it bouyed him to know that not everything he had done for his daughter had been taken away. Still, it didn't make it any easier to know it would be a long time before he saw her again, a longer time before he could really be a father to her.

Kurt stood at his daughter's bedside, staring down at the soft, round face. He reached for the tight curls on her head, feeling the baby-fine silkiness. It was suddenly difficult to breath, to swallow. He blinked rapidly to clear his eyes for this last sight of her.

"I love you," he whispered almost inaudibly. Seizing the moment her fear had never allowed him before, he bent and barely kissed her forehead, greedily breathing in that scent of her.

There would be a time, he told himself, when he would be able to do this with her awake. A time when he could read to her, take her to the park, the zoo, when she would run into his arms and hug him the way she did Stuart. There would be a time...

It was just going to take a while to happen.

Then he knew that if he didn't get the hell out of there now he was going to pick her up and run with her in spite of everything.

Stuart was waiting for him alone at the foot of the stairs when he came down. The shorter man extended his hand for the first time since they had met two and a half years ago and Kurt took it.

"I think this is the best thing for April. I just haven't had the guts to force the issue myself," Stuart said.

"Carol is too angry to tell you herself, but she'll comply."

"Good. And maybe since you realize it's necessary you'll oversee things and make sure of it."

"Carol really does love April," Stuart said in defense again.

"I hope she loves her enough to do what needs to be done. Because I meant everything I said."

Opening the door, Stuart merely nodded his head in acknowledgment.

There was no more to be said and with a last glance up the stairs toward April's room, Kurt left.

Driving back to the hotel he mulled over all that had happened and the fact that as difficult as it had been, as difficult as it would be to wait for the time when he would see April again, he knew he would be better off in the long run. But more had been accomplished today than that. In a roundabout way seeing April, Stuart and even Carol had led him to yet another decision, this one about Gillie.

The cold snap still had a grip on Colorado on Sunday morning as Gillie sat at her drawing table and watched the phone ring. She knew who it was. This was the third time Phil had called in the past hour. Elijah was next door at the Baumgardners' house so if he needed anything he would just run home. And no one but Phil let the phone ring so many times.

Twenty-five, twenty-six...

There was demand in that, Gillie realized. But then in the past three days since he had shown up on her doorstep, Phil was getting more demanding. He wanted her help and he wanted it right now. He didn't see any reason why she should need to think things over.

The phone was silent on the thirtieth ring and Gillie slumped over her drawing table, dropping her head on her crossed arms. She was so tired, physically and emotionally. Tired, frustrated, confused, guilty, angry...

"I'm a wreck," she said to herself, her voice echoing off the drawing she had been trying to do since five that morning. All she wanted was to turn the calendar back a month to before she had met Kurt Reynolds, before Phil Hunter had reappeared in her life. When things were serene. She and Elijah had been doing so well then.

When the doorbell rang she groaned. Robin had promised to keep Lijah there all day so Gillie could get some work done, but as contrary as her son had been in response to the turmoil of the last few days, he had already come back four times for things he absolutely couldn't stay over there without.

So much for trying to catch up on her work.

On the second ring of the doorbell Gillie pushed herself up slowly and met the green eyes of Kurt as he peered in the living-room window. Her breath caught at the first sight of him; joy and panic struck simultaneously. Here was the real reason handling the situation with Phil was taking such a toll on her. The real reason she couldn't sleep nights, couldn't work, couldn't think straight because of all the awful feelings that had a grip on her insides.

Again she had a flash of preference for serenity over the sublime, Kurt being the sublime. Serenity was a nice, trustworthy straight line. The sublime was a steep climb that led to a hard fall. A hard fall that hurt too much to make it all worth it.

She took a deep breath and climbed down from her stool, padding unenthusiastically to the front door. When she opened it Kurt already had the screen door open and was ready to come in.

"You look like hell, Hunter," he greeted her with affection in his voice, a smile on his lips and a frown pulling his brows together.

Then it's an improvement on how I feel, she thought, but all she said was, "Hello, Kurt."

He came in then and took his coat off, acting as if nothing had happened between them. He went into the kitchen, filled the kettle, set it to boil and took two cups from the cupboard. "Sit down. We need to talk," he informed her as he leaned against the counter.

It was on the tip of her tongue to ask if he didn't want to check under the bed or beat the bushes for that other man she was juggling, but she bit back the sarcasm and sat down. "How was your trip?" she asked dispiritedly, stiffly, as she took a chair.

"It was educational," he told her without hesitation.

The kettle whistled and Kurt turned his attention to making tea while Gillie stared at his back and hung on tightly to the anger and disillusionment that helped keep the lid on her feelings for him. A return to serenity was her goal, she reminded herself. Security and serenity that were only possible if she did a solo.

Kurt brought the tea to the table and sat. "Have you slept at all in the past three nights?"

Gillie shrugged. Since he was the cause, he was the last person she would admit it to. "I'm fine," she said militantly.

"Since the black car isn't out front I figured your ex-husband wasn't here. But where's Elijah?"

"Next door."

"And Phil?"

A part of Gillie acknowledged that it was said simply, matter-of-factly, while another part of her thought it rang with accusation. She raised her chin. "He's staying in the American Family Motel down by the highway."

Kurt nodded slowly. "Have you decided how you're going to help him?"

"I'm not sure yet. So far there's only been time to set him up in the motel, get him a haircut, get him to the doctor for a bad cough, and have his car heater fixed." This last came out tentatively, not so much because she didn't want Kurt to know but because she herself was suspicious of it. She hated herself for it, but couldn't help the doubts that request had raised. Without a place to stay Phil's car was his only form of shelter and warmth. She couldn't help wondering if a broken heater had inspired his return. She assumed her suspicions had been wrong since the heater had been fixed by late Friday afternoon and Phil not only hadn't disappeared but was still insistent that he wanted to clean up his act. And yet the doubts niggled, a reminder that she didn't trust him. That she shouldn't trust what anyone presented to her on the surface.

But Kurt didn't comment. Instead he said, "I found Carol inspiring as much tension as usual and April responding with the same elevated fear of me."

"I'm sorry," she said, meaning it.

"But thanks to you I talked to a psychologist before I left, so I went armed with what I think is the best way to handle it."

Gillie listened as he explained it all to her. She could see how difficult it was for him to accept an indefinite separation from the little girl and it weakened her control. She wanted to wrap her arms around him and comfort him. But she didn't. Instead she had a white-knuckled grip around her mug.

"It was pretty unnerving," he went on, "to find myself on friendly terms with Stuart. But more than that, it was bizarre to come away feeling a strong sense of gratitude to him of all people. Of feeling as if I'm indebted to him for loving April and raising her as if she's his own when I'm not allowed that privilege. If someone had told me I'd be feeling that to the man who helped destroy my marriage I would have laughed in his face. But there it is. And it made me realize that gratitude and debt can be strange things that are sometimes felt toward strange people in strange situations."

He paused a moment, staring at the steam rising from his cup. "I'm still not comfortable with you being around your ex-husband. I don't trust a man who has so far dealt with his problems the way he has. I don't trust his motives for being here, and I'm not as convinced as you are that he's harmless. But in Connecticut I realized two things, and one of them let me understand the obligation you feel toward him for what he did for you ten years ago. So like it or not, I'm here to tell you I can accept it.''

He took a sip of his tea, then went on. "The second thing I realized came from seeing Carol again and comparing the two of you. It occurred to me that the same integrity that makes you feel bound to pay that debt in a way that she doesn't even feel bound to encourage her own daughter to get over her fear of me as a stranger, is the same integrity that makes it ludicrous for me to believe you're doing it because of some hidden feelings for the man.'' He reached over and covered her hand with his. "And I'm sorry for having doubted you.''

The lure back to the sublime was strong. But equally as strong now was the reminder that what was on the surface for her to see was all too often not the truth. She forced herself to keep in mind that while this was the Kurt Reynolds she had thought him to be before—kind, understanding, compassionate, supportive—this was not what she had seen in him on Friday morning. And this could well be the facade.

Gillie pulled her hand out from under his and put it in her lap. "You're right. I'm not helping Phil because I love him and I would never *juggle men*.'' Saying that phrase put a little fire back into her convictions. It had particularly stung her, haunting her repeatedly since he had said it.

"Then accept my apology.''

"I do,'' she said blithely.

"But you don't forgive me.''

Gillie looked off over her shoulder. It wasn't easy not to forgive him, not to buy back into believing that he was wonderful and perfect. That was what she wanted to do. But alongside that desire was an old wound called disillusionment that was reopened and bleeding again. The pain of that was stronger and it left her more in need of the serenity than the sublime.

"Twice before I've been swept off my feet," she told him in a small voice because it was the best she could do around the constriction in her throat, in her heart. "Once by romance and once by kindness. Then you came along with both and woosh! I'm off my feet again. Trouble is, there always comes a time when I land flat on my face. And I just don't want to do that ever again."

"I love you, Gillie," he said, as if that should balance the scales. "I want you to marry me. I want you and me and Elijah to be a family."

Gillie just shook her head because she was fighting a flood of emotions that left her incapable of speaking.

"You're tired," he suggested.

She took a deep breath and sighed, forcing back the choked feeling in her throat. "You're right, I am. But that doesn't matter. This isn't coming out of fatigue. It's experience. I have to get things back to where they were before I met you. For my sake, for Elijah's. We were happy, our life was settled. It can't be that way with a man in it, with me always waiting for the other shoe to drop."

"There is no other shoe to drop."

"Isn't there? I know your relationships with kids are good. Great, in fact. I know how much you love your daughter and that for her you've done something selfless, generous and that's difficult for you. But I'm not a child and when it comes to adult relationships, I just don't believe what you see is what you get. What I got on Friday was certainly not what I've seen before. And I don't want any more surprises in my life."

"I know I was unreasonable on Friday. I flew off the handle. But that was a reaction, not evidence of a darker side of me."

"I've learned that that's where reactions come from. They're the only warning signs we get and they shouldn't be ignored."

"What do you think I'm hiding?" he shouted suddenly, frustration sounding in his voice.

"I've also learned that there's no way of telling that until it surfaces," she said fatalistically. "And once it does it never goes away. It stays to make life hell."

"I'm not hiding any dark side, for crying out loud."

His anger sparked her own. "Aren't you? If you had been everything you led your wife to believe you were she wouldn't have left."

"Low blow," he told her gravely. "My wife had her own agenda. I never misled her, she misled me. And what about you?" he shot back verbally. "You weren't totally honest with me. I had no idea in the world that Elijah was fathered by someone else, that you were carrying around a feeling of debt to the man who had bailed you out. That doesn't mean I think there are some other secrets in your past or some hideous flaws in your character. And I'd be a jackass if I did."

"So you think I'm a jackass because I do wonder what's really behind the polished front that's there for me to see? Well, you're wrong. I was a jackass twice before for overlooking the signs that did show up. But I'm not a jackass anymore. The only way Elijah and I can be safe is to stay alone. And that's what I intend to do."

"I don't suppose it occurred to you that it may be safe but it isn't healthy, not for you or for Elijah. Your idea of being safe is to write off life, to cut you both off from what we all need—other people, intimacy, love, companionship. If it was working out so damn well before then why was Elijah in trouble all the time? Why did he need me in the first place? And what about you? Doing nothing but going through the motions of living. Working, eating, sleeping, working, eating, sleeping. Never stepping beyond the boundaries of your cocoon. Eight years without so much as having a man touch you. That's not being settled, Gillie, that's just this side of being dead. And what is it teaching Elijah about how to live his own life? About the relationships a man and woman can have? For both of your sakes, come back to the land of the living."

Full-blown anger felt better than the pain of denying what her heart wanted. Gillie grabbed hold of it and held on tight. "What phenomenal egotism to think that Elijah and I have no life without you. I beg your pardon, but we were happy and content. Yes he had some problems at school, but not because *you* weren't on the scene. It's a stage he's going through and he'll outgrow it. You were just a different channeling of that energy, not his savior. And you aren't mine, either. I may have been in need of being rescued once before in my life, but no more. I am completely capable of handling everything I need to handle and having a full life on my own."

"If you're so strong and self-sufficient then why was I blown out of the water on Friday because you expected my help and support and didn't think I was giving it?"

"The operative word is *expected*. Because you led me to believe that you were the kind of person I could expect help and support from, not because I *needed* it. What you were 'blown out of the water for' was showing me a glimpse of what was—or wasn't—behind it."

He looked up at the ceiling and shook his head. "This is ridiculous," he murmured.

"It isn't ridiculous. It's over," she said in the heat of the moment.

Silence fell, so full of tension it was palpable.

Then Kurt said, "That's how you want it?"

"That's how I want it."

His eyes pierced her for a moment. Gillie looked away to tell him she was impervious to him.

"Fine," he said, standing. "Have it your way."

Gillie didn't watch as he walked off. She didn't so much as blink when she heard him yank the front door open. But the sound of it slamming closed behind him cracked the shield of her anger and let loose a flood of agony.

"No, it's more than fine," she said in the stillness that followed the sound of his car wheels screeching up the street. "It's the only way to be sure."

Chapter Twelve

This one is going to cost you," Gillie told her son as she led him into the house on Monday after being called to the elementary school and picking him up.

Elijah stormed passed her, every bit as mad as she, his chin tucked, his eyes narrowed, and his shoulders hunched. His lack of contrition only fueled Gillie's anger. She took a deep breath and counted to ten.

When she spoke again her voice was barely controlled. "What I want to know is how you even knew what to do to cause the toilet in the women's restroom to squirt up like a geyser when it was flushed."

Elijah shrugged and mumbled his answer. "Matt's big brother showed me."

"Matt's big brother," Gillie repeated in a continuing effort to keep a grip on her temper. "In the first place, it's outrageous that you did such a thing at all.

What if you had done serious damage to the school plumbing? Do you have any idea what something like that costs?'' The battle was lost—she railed at him. Then she decided maybe it was for the best to scare him. Nothing else she had done in the past week in response to the worst behavior the ten-year-old had ever exhibited had had any effect. "Do you realize it could be considered vandalism and you could be arrested?''

"What do you care? You're busy with *that guy*," he muttered under his breath.

Gillie prayed for patience and resisted reprimanding him for what would have been the hundredth time about how disrespectful it was to refer to Phil as *that guy*, the only thing Elijah ever called him.

The ten-year-old sighed and said snidely, "Can I have a snack now?''

"No, you can't have a snack now," Gillie shouted. "In fact your snacks are reduced to nothing but a glass of milk for the next week. You will also have no desserts and you will use your allowance to pay the cleaning bill for the music teacher's dress.''

The boy's head came up. "I already have detention for a week. It's not fair that I should have to do anything else.''

"Not fair? The music teacher wanted you suspended from school. If Bob hadn't calmed her down you'd be in even worse shape. You ought to consider yourself lucky to have gotten off this easy. Now get your milk and go to your room.''

"Fine," he shouted back. "I'd rather go to my room than stay out here with you. Ever since that guy came around here you baby him and take your bad mood out on me.''

Gillie saw red. She held her arm out and pointed down the hall. "You've just lost the milk. Now get your fanny into your room."

Elijah sulked off, slamming his door in final protest.

Gillie closed her eyes and shook her head. "I should have been a nun."

Just then the front doorbell rang and her heart lurched—the same response it had been giving to every ring of the phone or doorbell since Kurt had walked out. Of course there was no reason to think it would be him. Of course she didn't want it to be him. Of course if it was him she would just turn him away again. But still the thought was there in her mind until the moment she opened the door and found Robin's sympathetic face on the other side. Also involuntarily, that same lurching heart sank to her toes.

With her ever-present coffee cup in hand, Robin came in. "Bob just called and told me about your son the plumber. Thought I'd see if you need help killing him."

"Tempting. But if I wanted him murdered I would have just left him to the music teacher." Gillie fell into the recliner, arms and legs splayed, chin on her chest.

Robin perched on the edge of the coffee table. "Phil called my house looking for you while you were at the school."

Gillie's head shot up. When she hadn't answered his fifth call the day before he had phoned the Baumgardners' to find out where she was. It was effective. After that Gillie had felt as if she had no choice but to answer her phone so that he didn't bother other people. It really rubbed her the wrong way to be manipulated. She hadn't told him that, but she had asked him not to bother Robin. Obviously her request had had no impact. "I'm sorry," she said to her cousin.

"He's really badgering you, isn't he?"

Gillie took a deep breath and sighed. "He doesn't like staying in a motel. He says he needs someplace homey to live while he goes through this. He needs concentrated help and support, someone to be there for him regardless of the time of day or night, not to be exiled and left alone. He says if I just give him six months he'll be back on his feet and I won't ever have to see him again."

This time it was Robin who took a deep breath, but hers sounded disgusted. "Six months of what you've been doing—calling doctors for him, taking him everywhere he needs to go, trying to find out what kind of benefits he has coming, how to get financial aid, bringing his meals, washing his clothes, footing the bills and holding his hand. Seems to me that he's asking an awful lot."

Gillie decided it was exhausting just talking about it. She changed the subject. "Did Bob have any suggestions about Kurt—I mean about Elijah?"

One of Robin's eyebrows jumped up. "No, he didn't have any suggestions about Elijah or Kurt. But I have one about Kurt."

"I know, you told me last night."

"When I found you in here sobbing your eyes out. You're out of your mind if you let him go."

"These days I am definitely feeling out of my mind. And he's already been let go. No ifs about it. I can't handle waiting to be bitten by what's really behind the perfect and wonderful front.''

''Perfect and wonderful? Hmm. So that's how you saw him. Well, I agree that he's wonderful. But nobody's perfect,'' Robin said pointedly. ''Since it didn't work out, though, I have a new client I want you to meet.''

That made Gillie laugh mirthlessly. ''Don't you even think about it. No way. Start the matchmaking stuff on me again and I swear I'll disown you.''

''Then call Kurt and tell him you're a knucklehead who's been under so much pressure that you weren't seeing things clearly.''

Gillie groaned. ''You know I love you, Robin, but will you go home?''

Robin stood up. ''I'm telling you, when this whole thing is over with Phil—even if it is six months from now—and you're thinking straight again, you're going to be one sorry lady that Kurt is nowhere around.''

''I'll remember you said so. But for now would you just leave me alone?''

''Okay,'' Robin said resignedly on her way out. ''If you need me, call.''

When the door closed after her cousin, Gillie let her chin drop back down to her chest. She didn't want to think about anything at all so she closed her eyes and counted her breaths. She made it to five before her thoughts wandered.

For the first time since Phil had appeared on her doorstep something stuck in her mind and wouldn't dislodge—Elijah's comment about her babying Phil.

She had believed that Elijah's recent bad behavior was a response to the tension in their lives lately. But maybe that was only partially true.

Did she inspire resentment in her son by treating Phil like a new baby?

It was an angle Gillie had to think about for a moment. She walked on eggs with her ex-husband, she catered to him, she coddled him, she excused him, she buckled in to his demands and let his behavior manipulate her.

"That's babying him, all right," she mumbled disdainfully to herself. "And it's the way a bad mother would do it."

A good mother, she knew, helped her child to help himself and stand on his own two feet. She gave her child the tools to use in dealing with problems, but she didn't solve them for him. What she had been doing with Phil Hunter was bad parenting. What he wanted of her, what she had been giving and was considering giving even more of, would cripple a child.

Certainly it could do Phil no good, either.

It suddenly occurred to her that repaying a debt sometimes took a form other than what was asked as repayment.

"Elijah, get your coat on," she hollered to her son. "I'm going to need you to stay next door for a while."

It was dark by the time Gillie got to the motel where her ex-husband was staying. She parked directly in front of his room. The lights were on but since his car wasn't outside she turned her ignition off and settled in to wait for him. Just as she did his door opened and, with ice bucket in hand, Phil stepped out, saw her and stopped in his tracks.

Gillie took a breath and steeled herself for what she was about to do.

"Hi," he greeted, smiling at her as she got out of her car and went toward him. He looked as if he had aged fifteen years in the last five. For the first time since he had re-entered her life it struck Gillie that his eyes were still the bluest she had ever seen and that made her very sad, as if his beautiful blue eyes were a reminder of all of the potential he hadn't lived up to.

"Where's your car?" Gillie asked as she followed him into the brightly lit motel room.

"I, uh, sold it," he said, looking away from her and setting the ice bucket beside an unopened bottle of cheap whiskey.

"You sold it?" Gillie repeated neutrally.

"Thought I'd need the money more than the car. I figured you'd come through for me, and I was thinking that I could use the money toward a little trailer that I could park on the side of your house to live out of. You've been taking me wherever I need to go anyway, so it wasn't like I had to have it for transportation. Did you get the information on programs for vets?"

"No, I didn't. But I do have something to tell you."

He seemed to deflate before her eyes, as if he sensed what she was going to say. He raked one hand through his hair and Gillie's gaze caught on a hole in the underarm of his sleeve. For some reason that brought a flash of memory of the way he had looked when she had first met him all those years ago. He had been dressed in jeans and a plaid flannel shirt then, too, but unlike now both had been crisp and new, his cowboy boots polished to a gloss.

Again a wave of sadness washed over her, but this time it brought with it the realization that what she felt for him was what she would feel for any other human being who had hit bottom, that she didn't feel plugged into that same plight the way she had when they had been married and again when he had first come to call in the debt she owed him.

Gillie took a deep breath for courage and said, "I've made my decision about helping you."

"And you aren't going to," he finished with a note of accusation in his voice.

"Not the way you want me to, no. It won't do you any good for me to be your crutch, Phil."

"It did you some good for me to be yours."

He sounded like a disappointed little boy and it lent weight to Gillie's determination, reaffirming what she had just come to understand about the structure of their relationship being one of parent-child. "I've called the veteran's hospital in Virginia," she told him rather than argue about what she owed him. "I know you can't do this alone, and with your family there you would have all the support you need. The hospital has several programs that are just what you said you wanted—"

That was as far as she got before he cut her off. "So you're pawning me off on my family."

"I'm giving you what you gave me, Phil—a fresh start," she told him calmly, but not easily, then went on to elaborate her new position.

She let her words sink in for a moment before continuing. "I have a plane ticket here for a flight out in three hours. I'll take you to the airport if you'll go, but that's all I'll do. Whether you take my offer and go, or you just cash in the ticket and stay, you're on your own from here.''

He turned his back to her and hunched over, his hands on a small table to brace himself. She saw his head shake back and forth, she heard him sigh, a short gust of air from his nose.

Gillie recognized the feelings his response sent through her; they were the same as when she watched her son struggle with something he thought was bigger than he. She knew the urge to charge in and rescue. And she knew she had to resist it.

Then Phil pushed himself up and faced her again. ''I'll get my stuff packed while you check me out. We might as well head to the airport right now.''

For a moment Gillie stared at him as if she hadn't heard him right. Then she shook herself out of her stupor. ''Good,'' was all she said.

At Stapleton International Airport she carried one grocery sack of his belongings while he carried the other and when the airlines refused to check them, she bought a duffle bag and they transferred all of his worldly possessions into it so he wouldn't have to take them on the plane with him.

Just as it was time to board, Phil turned to her with a smile that seemed to reflect all of the sadness she had been feeling for him.

''You didn't expect me to accept this, did you?'' he asked.

Gillie only shrugged.

Phil laughed a little ruefully. ''You didn't believe I was really serious about going straight this time. I knew it all along. I could see in your face that you were waiting for something to prove I didn't mean what I said. You kept watching, asking questions that made me know you figured any minute now I was just going to rip you off and disappear like before. Not that I haven't earned it, but that much suspicion is a bad thing, Gil." Then he touched his temple with the plane ticket in a little salute. "Take care."

"You, too. Good luck." She watched him disappear down the loading tunnel, feeling certain she had done the right thing, the best thing for Phil.

Then she went home to embrace the serenity she so desperately needed.

In the week that followed, Gillie's life went back to normal but somehow it didn't seem serene. It just seemed empty. And in that emptiness were constant thoughts of Kurt and the echo of Phil's words.

The image of herself as a suspicious person was not one she particularly liked, and yet there was no denying it. Regardless of how she had defended Phil to Kurt, claimed she believed that this time was different and that he was sincere, she'd still had doubts that it wasn't true. Why else had she thought once his car heater was fixed he would disappear? Why else had she been shocked when he had so easily accepted her offer? Phil was right, though, he *had* earned her distrust. Years of bad behavior, of the worst always happening, had definitely earned him suspicions.

But had it earned Kurt a dose of the same suspicions? she began to wonder. Because that was what he had gotten. At the first sign that he was going to disappoint her, even though it was nowhere near the scope of how Phil or Paul had disappointed her, that he wasn't going to live up to her expectations, she had been convinced that it was an indication of a darker side that was his true nature.

Had she blurred all the men in her life together? It seemed possible, she had to admit. And the more she thought about it, the more it seemed that Kurt had taken the shell fragments thrown off by those other two bombs in her past. Because of that and because her heart felt as if it had taken up permanent residence in her throat, she decided that maybe she should take a second look at some things, beginning with her own expectations.

After two seriously flawed men in her life before him, Kurt had seemed perfect. *Seemed* perfect. He hadn't pretended to be. He hadn't hidden things about himself the way Phil had.

But he wasn't perfect. He had shocked her by withholding support and understanding when she had expected him to lavish it.

"And what about you, Gil?" she asked herself as she lay in bed Thursday night, unable to sleep for the heavy depression that had settled in. "How understanding were you?" Knowing the circumstances that had destroyed his marriage, shouldn't she have been just a little understanding of his sensitivity to another man in her life?

"Okay, so I'm not perfect, either."

But no matter how she looked at it, how much she didn't want to be a suspicious person, she was still scared that there was another side of Kurt that could hurt her as badly as she had been hurt before.

How could she tell?

Something inside her told her that with Kurt, what she saw was what she would get. It was only an instinct, but maybe it was time to go with a good instinct instead of going against bad ones.

"The bottom line," she whispered to herself in the dark, "is that I want him enough to trust him *and* my instincts this time." Because her love for him was stronger than anything else. Stronger than her fear, stronger than her suspicions and her doubts, stronger than she was.

Gillie borrowed Robin's typewriter, briefcase, a business suit and an overcoat as soon as she came back from taking Elijah to school on Friday. When the doors to the shopping mall opened she was waiting with charge card at the ready and determination in her heart. It took only half an hour to find what she wanted. Then she went home and spent the day hunting and pecking on the typewriter for two pages before taking a long, perfumed bath, washing her hair, curling it and fussing over her makeup until it was just right.

With Robin picking Elijah up from school, Gillie had planned on leaving the house by three so she would be waiting in the parking lot the minute Kurt got home. But one look at herself in the full-length mirror in her morning's purchase and panic struck.

"Please God, don't let me be making a fool out of myself," she said as she slipped on Robin's large suit.

It was after four before she could make herself leave, and her hand was shaking so badly she had trouble getting the key in the ignition of her car.

What if it was too late? What if he didn't want her anymore?

It had begun to snow lightly; powdery flakes hit her windshield and melted. The defroster was on full-blast and Gillie could still hear the beat of her own heart over the sound.

His car was in the parking lot; she pulled into the spot beside it. But Gillie just sat there trying to breathe. Her lungs seemed to have forgotten how.

What would the radio shrink have to say about this?

We all have to face the consequences of our actions.

But what if the consequences were that Kurt was newly convinced that *he* was safer solo?

The car interior grew cold and a shiver shook her. It was either go inside or turn the motor back on for some heat. Gillie decided to get it over with.

At the building's entrance she pushed the button above his name on the mailbox. Then she waited, understanding first-hand the term bated breath. But there was no answer.

Had Kurt seen her car? Did he know it was her? Did he not want to see her?

Her pulse rate seemed to double and Gillie wondered if she was going to have a heart attack standing there.

"Ad Artist Keels Over On Lover's Landing."

For a moment she thought of going home. Of giving up. He must have seen her car, and since he didn't want anything to do with a suspicious woman he wasn't going to let her in.

But she didn't like being a suspicious person. She was working on that. Give him the benefit of the doubt, she urged herself, then pushed the button again.

This time Kurt's voice came over the intercom.

"Who is it?" he demanded, none too friendly, and again Gillie wondered if he knew it was her.

"It's me," she said in a voice she wasn't sure was loud enough for him to hear, and then added inanely, "Gillie."

Again nothing happened. There was no answer over the intercom, the security door didn't buzz open.

He didn't want to see her. It was over. She'd blown it.

Then a sound like a buzz saw broke the silence and Gillie lunged for the knob as if it might stop before she got the door open.

Suddenly Gillie's legs seemed too heavy to lift onto that first step. Then she heard Kurt's apartment door open on the third floor and she forced herself to climb the stairs, feeling as if it was the steepest mountain in the world.

His expression was not warm or welcoming when she first caught sight of it through the balustrade poles on the last flight. She reminded herself that she was approaching this in a businesslike fashion and squared her shoulders.

"Gillie," he greeted, part-questioning, part-challenging statement. Then he stepped back to allow her in.

His coat was hanging on the hall tree, his tie and suit jacket were slung over the back of the couch. Gillie thought it was easier to look at these things than at him. Then, without taking her own coat off, she went to set her briefcase on the coffee table, snapping it open officiously.

"If we were married I'd say you were serving me with divorce papers," he said sardonically, coming to stand in front of her.

Straightening, Gillie couldn't avoid looking at him. His expression was confused and stern, and there were shadows under his eyes that matched hers. She swallowed and held out her two typewritten pages.

"What's this?" he asked with the arch of one brow.

She had to clear her throat to get words out. "My résumé," she told him in a voice that was smaller and less confident than she had intended.

"Your résumé." His glance went to the sheets extended to him and then to her face, but he didn't accept them. "Your *personal* résumé?"

"I'm submitting it."

"Why?"

Gillie had to ask herself the same thing at the sound of anger in his tone.

Before she could respond, he went on. "It's you who has a need for it, not me. Or are there more skeletons in your closet?"

"Maybe I shouldn't have come," she said, beginning to pull the papers back. Before she could, he took them from her.

"Why exactly did you come?" he asked as he glanced down at what he held.

"I..." She had to clear her throat yet again. Had his attitude been different it might not have been so hard to answer. But as it was, exposing any more seemed foolhardy.

Suspicious person. The title taunted her. He isn't perfect, she reminded herself. He had good reason not to welcome her with open arms.

"I've been thinking things over and I was unfair to you," she managed to say. "You got some fallout you didn't deserve."

"Meaning?" He didn't look up from what he was reading.

"I made a bigger deal out of what happened between us than I should have. But at the time I lost sight of how you would naturally feel about another man in my life . . . in my house—"

"In a towel," he added.

"I was in such a muddle, there were so many alarms going off in my head and on top of it you took me by surprise by not just jumping into my problems with both feet. I guess I—"

"Thought the worst," he finished, putting the first sheet behind the second and continuing to read.

"I thought you were perfect," she said feebly.

That brought his head up, his green eyes piercing her from beneath a frown.

But Gillie hurried on before he could say anything. "I know it wasn't as if you worked to give me that impression the way Phil did to cover up his problems. It's just that that was what I thought."

"I'm not perfect by a long shot."

"You're a lot closer to being perfect than any man I've ever had in my life." The words slipped out wryly.

Kurt lifted the papers in her direction. "I'm unprepared. I don't have one of these to offer you in return."

"I guess I'll just have to trust you."

"Do you?" He sounded dubious.

"Yes," she answered without hesitation. "It was you who talked about instincts before, about trusting yours. It just took me a little longer to get to that same place."

"Meaning that now your instincts about me, about us, are good when before they were bad?" His green eyes stayed on her.

"They were never bad," she admitted. "I was just too suspicious to accept them, and you, without doubting."

He nodded his head slowly, watching her all the while. After a moment he said, "And what about your ex-husband? Where does he fit into the future?"

Gillie pointed to the papers with her chin. "That's the last part." She explained what ended her résumé, complete with how she put Phil on the plane on Monday night. "It was a comment Phil made that started me realizing just how suspicious I was . . . and how unfounded my suspicion was when it came to you. He had earned it, you see, and when I thought about that, it occurred to me that you hadn't."

"So you came here in that getup to let me know you're all business and to submit your personal résumé. Why?" he repeated yet again.

"Because I love you, Kurt," she told him softly, praying she wasn't laying bare her soul to a man who had written her off.

"How much?" he demanded curtly.

"A lot."

He shot out questions like a drill sergeant. "Enough to let me be a full part of your life? Enough to marry me? Enough to let me adopt Elijah and be his honest-to-God father?''

Hope made Gillie lightheaded. "Yes."

The drill sergeant mellowed slightly. "Enough not to think that every time I blow my stack or leave dirty socks on the floor I'm turning from Dr. Jekyll into Mr. Hyde?"

That made her smile and it felt good. "Yes."

He tossed the papers onto the couch and pulled her roughly into his arms. "Come here," he said raggedly as he held her tightly. He sighed into her hair, a long, deep release. "You're a little slow in coming around," he criticized. "But since I'm in love with you I guess I'll just have to accept your faults."

Gillie wrapped her arms around his waist and burrowed against his body. "Do you love me enough to know that I would never cheat on you?" she demanded the way he had.

"Yes," he answered with a little laugh in his voice. "But too much to ever find a man in a towel anywhere near you ever again."

She tilted her head back to look up at him. "That towel really bothered you, didn't it?"

"You'll never know." He peered down at her suspiciously. "Speaking of towels, what's under this trench coat?"

"One of Robin's business suits," she said with so much mock innocence it was clear that wasn't all.

"And what's under Robin's business suit?"

Gillie shrugged and settled her cheek against his chest again. "Guess you'll have to find out."

"I see. You were figuring that if your résumé didn't get you the job your underwear might."

"Something like that."

But he didn't make a move to explore. Instead he stayed holding her.

"Aren't you even curious?" she asked after a while.

"I'm savoring," he said reverently. "I've spent the last week so far down I was looking up at hell because I didn't think this was ever going to happen again."

"I'm sorry," she whispered, unable to convey just how deeply in those two words.

"I think we ought to explain everything about his fathers to Elijah when we tell him about us, about my wanting to adopt him."

"Everything?"

"Everything. I think he's old enough to understand; he's a sharp kid. And I want him to know all the facts so we don't have any more of the past hanging over our heads."

"All right."

"I want to pick him up in about two hours, go to dinner and then tell him the whole thing. Then I want the three of us to make wedding plans."

"But not for two hours? What are we going to do in the meantime?" she asked hopefully.

"How'd you go eight years before?" he teased, solemnity leaving his voice for the first time.

"I've been wondering that same thing."

"I love you, Gillie," he said again. "We're going to have the rest of our lives together. And the only true color you'll ever see under the surface is the most stubborn determination in the world never to let you or Elijah go."

"I can live with that."

He laughed, a full-throated, deep baritone sound that she could listen to for the rest of her life. "I only have one thing to tell you in place of my own résumé."

"I hope it's fast," she said because it didn't matter to her anymore; the past was over with for them both.

"I've never in my life loved a woman more than I love you."

"Prove it," she said, her tone relaying how much that touched her.

He took her hand and pulled her into the bedroom. "I'd be happy to."

*   *   *   *   *

COMING NEXT MONTH

#559 YESTERDAY'S CHILD—Diana Whitney
Leah Wainwright and Boyd Cauldwell had been childhood sweethearts—
until Leah's mysterious disappearance amid whispered rumors. Years
later, Leah suddenly returned, youngster in tow, and a dangerous flame
was about to be rekindled.

#560 A MAN WITH SECRETS—Sondra Stanford
Despite her deep suspicions, Alissa Comier Browning couldn't deny her
desperate attraction to Rafferty Stone. Then she discovered that Raff was
indeed a man with secrets....

#561 THE PERFECT LOVER—Jessica St. James
Romance editor Hannah Grant was the ultimate dreamer; Rook
McAllister was a solid realist. When their worlds collided, all hell broke
loose—in a heavenly tangle of lassos and limos, mayhem and miracles.

#562 GODDESS OF JOY—Bevlyn Marshall
Holly Murphey feared it was her prized figurine—not her love—that
collector Philip Irons so intensely desired. Could he ever convince her that
she was his true goddess of joy?

#563 HIGH STAKES—Dana Warren Smith
Wealthy, sheltered Jamie Logan dated backwoods farmer Ren Garrett on a
bet. But soon the stakes shot sky-high, and the jackpot was love!

#564 GAMES OF CHANCE—Laurey Bright
Pilot Jacqueline Renton had learned to be tough, self-sufficient and
unsentimental. A mercy mission threatened to reopen the door to her
heart—while compassionate Dr. Finn Simonson waited to stride right in.

Available this month:

You'll flip . . . your pages won't!
Read paperbacks *hands-free* with

Book Mate • I

The perfect "mate" for all your romance paperbacks

Traveling • Vacationing • At Work • In Bed • Studying • Cooking • Eating

Perfect size for all standard paperbacks, this wonderful invention makes reading a pure pleasure! Ingenious design holds paperback books OPEN and FLAT so even wind can't ruffle pages – leaves your hands free to do other things. Reinforced, wipe-clean vinyl-covered holder flexes to let you turn pages without undoing the strap . . . supports paperbacks so well, they have the strength of hardcovers!

Pages turn WITHOUT opening the strap.

SEE-THROUGH STRAP

Reinforced back stays flat.

Built in bookmark

BOOK MARK

BACK COVER HOLDING STRIP

10˝ x 7¼˝ , opened.
Snaps closed for easy carrying, too

INDULGE A LITTLE SWEEPSTAKES

OFFICIAL RULES

SWEEPSTAKES RULES AND REGULATIONS. NO PURCHASE NECESSARY.

1. NO PURCHASE NECESSARY. To enter complete the official entry form and return with the invoice in the envelope provided. Or you may enter by printing your name, complete address and your daytime phone number on a 3 x 5 piece of paper. Include with your entry the hand printed words "Indulge A Little Sweepstakes." Mail your entry to: Indulge A Little Sweepstakes, P.O. Box 1397, Buffalo, NY 14269-1397. No mechanically reproduced entries accepted. Not responsible for late, lost, misdirected mail, or printing errors.

2. Three winners, one per month (Sept. 30, 1989, October 31, 1989 and November 30, 1989), will be selected in random drawings. All entries received prior to the drawing date will be eligible for that month's prize. This sweepstakes is under the supervision of MARDEN-KANE, INC. an independent judging organization whose decisions are final and binding. Winners will be notified by telephone and may be required to execute an affidavit of eligibility and release which must be returned within 14 days, or an alternate winner will be selected.

3. Prizes: 1st Grand Prize (1) a trip for two to Disneyworld in Orlando, Florida. Trip includes round trip air transportation, hotel accommodations for seven days and six nights, plus up to $700 expense money (ARV $3,500). 2nd Grand Prize (1) a seven-night Chandris Caribbean Cruise for two includes transportation from nearest major airport, accommodations, meals plus up to $1,000 in expense money (ARV $4,300). 3rd Grand Prize (1) a ten-day Hawaiian holiday for two includes round trip air transportation for two, hotel accommodations, sightseeing, plus up to $1,200 in spending money (ARV $7,700). All trips subject to availability and must be taken as outlined on the entry form.

4. Sweepstakes open to residents of the U.S. and Canada 18 years or older except employees and the families of Torstar Corp., its affiliates, subsidiaries and Marden-Kane, Inc. and all other agencies and persons connected with conducting this sweepstakes. All Federal, State and local laws and regulations apply. Void wherever prohibited or restricted by law. Taxes, if any are the sole responsibility of the prize winners. Canadian winners will be required to answer a skill testing question. Winners consent to the use of their name, photograph and/or likeness for publicity purposes without additional compensation.

5. For a list of prize winners, send a stamped, self-addressed envelope to Indulge A Little Sweepstakes Winners, P.O. Box 701, Sayreville, NJ 08871.

DL-SWPS

INDULGE A LITTLE SWEEPSTAKES

OFFICIAL RULES

SWEEPSTAKES RULES AND REGULATIONS. NO PURCHASE NECESSARY.

1. NO PURCHASE NECESSARY. To enter complete the official entry form and return with the invoice in the envelope provided. Or you may enter by printing your name, complete address and your daytime phone number on a 3 x 5 piece of paper. Include with your entry the hand printed words "Indulge A Little Sweepstakes." Mail your entry to: Indulge A Little Sweepstakes, P.O. Box 1397, Buffalo, NY 14269-1397. No mechanically reproduced entries accepted. Not responsible for late, lost, misdirected mail, or printing errors.

2. Three winners, one per month (Sept. 30, 1989, October 31, 1989 and November 30, 1989), will be selected in random drawings. All entries received prior to the drawing date will be eligible for that month's prize. This sweepstakes is under the supervision of MARDEN-KANE, INC. an independent judging organization whose decisions are final and binding. Winners will be notified by telephone and may be required to execute an affidavit of eligibility and release which must be returned within 14 days, or an alternate winner will be selected.

3. Prizes: 1st Grand Prize (1) a trip for two to Disneyworld in Orlando, Florida. Trip includes round trip air transportation, hotel accommodations for seven days and six nights, plus up to $700 expense money (ARV $3,500). 2nd Grand Prize (1) a seven-night Chandris Caribbean Cruise for two includes transportation from nearest major airport, accommodations, meals plus up to $1,000 in expense money (ARV $4,300). 3rd Grand Prize (1) a ten-day Hawaiian holiday for two includes round trip air transportation for two, hotel accommodations, sightseeing, plus up to $1,200 in spending money (ARV $7,700). All trips subject to availability and must be taken as outlined on the entry form.

4. Sweepstakes open to residents of the U.S. and Canada 18 years or older except employees and the families of Torstar Corp., its affiliates, subsidiaries and Marden-Kane, Inc. and all other agencies and persons connected with conducting this sweepstakes. All Federal, State and local laws and regulations apply. Void wherever prohibited or restricted by law. Taxes, if any are the sole responsibility of the prize winners. Canadian winners will be required to answer a skill testing question. Winners consent to the use of their name, photograph and/or likeness for publicity purposes without additional compensation.

5. For a list of prize winners, send a stamped, self-addressed envelope to Indulge A Little Sweepstakes Winners, P.O. Box 701, Sayreville, NJ 08871.

© 1989 HARLEQUIN ENTERPRISES LTD.

DL-SWPS

INDULGE A LITTLE—WIN A LOT!

Summer of '89 Subscribers-Only Sweepstakes

OFFICIAL ENTRY FORM

This entry must be received by: Sept. 30, 1989
This month's winner will be notified by: October 7, 1989
Trip must be taken between: Nov. 7, 1989–Nov. 7, 1990

YES, I want to win the Walt Disney World® vacation for two! I understand the prize includes round-trip airfare, first-class hotel, and a daily allowance as revealed on the "Wallet" scratch-off card.

Name_____

Address_____

City_____State/Prov._____Zip/Postal Code_____

Daytime phone number_____
Area code

Return entries with invoice in envelope provided. Each book in this shipment has two entry coupons—and the more coupons you enter, the better your chances of winning!
© 1989 HARLEQUIN ENTERPRISES LTD.

DINDL-1

INDULGE A LITTLE—WIN A LOT!

Summer of '89 Subscribers-Only Sweepstakes

OFFICIAL ENTRY FORM

This entry must be received by: Sept. 30, 1989
This month's winner will be notified by: October 7, 1989
Trip must be taken between: Nov. 7, 1989–Nov. 7, 1990

YES, I want to win the Walt Disney World® vacation for two! I understand the prize includes round-trip airfare, first-class hotel, and a daily allowance as revealed on the "Wallet" scratch-off card.

Name_____

Address_____

City_____State/Prov._____Zip/Postal Code_____

Daytime phone number_____
Area code

Return entries with invoice in envelope provided. Each book in this shipment has two entry coupons—and the more coupons you enter, the better your chances of winning!
© 1989 HARLEQUIN ENTERPRISES LTD.

DINDL-1